Christmas Memories at Grace Chapel Inn

Christmas Memories at Grace Chapel Inn

New York, New York

Christmas Memories at Grace Chapel Inn

ISBN-13: 978-0-8249-4507-7

Published by Guideposts
16 East 34th Street
New York, New York 10016
Guideposts.org

Distributed by Ideals Publications, a Guideposts company
2630 Elm Hill Pike, Suite 100
Nashville, TN 37214

Guideposts and *Ideals* are registered trademarks of Guideposts.

The characters and events in this book are fictional, and any resemblance
to actual persons or events is coincidental.

Scripture references are from the following sources: The Holy Bible, King James
Version (KJV). The Holy Bible, New International Version®, NIV®. Copyright
© 1973, 1978, 1984 by Biblica, Inc.™ Used by permission of Zondervan. All
rights reserved worldwide.

Library of Congress Cataloging-in-Publication Data has been applied for.

Cover illustration by Deborah Chabrian
Interior design by Marisa Jackson
Typeset by Müllerhaus Publishing Group | www.mullerhaus.net

Printed and bound in the United States of America
10 9 8 7 6 5 4 3 2 1

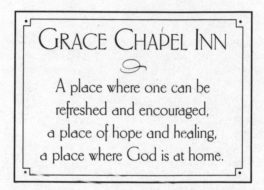

GRACE CHAPEL INN

A place where one can be
refreshed and encouraged,
a place of hope and healing,
a place where God is at home.

$\mathcal{T}$hat was a wonderful dinner, ladies. Thank you for including me in your Christmas Eve." Grace Chapel's Pastor Kenneth Thompson looked handsome and festive with a red sweater beneath his gray pinstripe suit. His comment was followed by a chorus of compliments from the group gathered with him at the front door of Grace Chapel Inn. Assistant Pastor Henry Ley and his wife Patsy, Jane's best friend Sylvia Songer, Mayor Lloyd Tynan, and the Howard sisters' aunt Ethel Buckley all thanked the sisters for their hospitality.

A long swag of fresh evergreens intertwined with gold ribbon and small brass bells outlined the doorway. The bells tinkled merrily as the door opened. "We're glad you could come. Merry Christmas," Louise Smith said. Her sisters, Jane and Alice Howard, echoed her wishes as everyone hugged, and the group walked out into the starlit night, crunching through the new fallen snow.

"What a feast!" Louise's daughter Cynthia exclaimed.

"Yes, Jane, that was a marvelous dinner," Alice said with a soft smile. "It reminded me of Christmas Eve when Mother was alive. Was that her recipe?"

"Yes. I found it in her cookbook. It was her seafood thermidor. She'd written 'Christmas Eve Dinner' above the recipe." Jane had been a professional chef before she moved back home to Acorn Hill, and she was always on the lookout for new and unusual recipes to try.

"I thought so, although I don't believe she used lobster meat. That would have been too rich for her budget. Shrimp or crabmeat made it special back then."

"The lobster was compliments of a couple from Maine who stayed here last month," Louise explained to Cynthia. The three sisters ran a bed-and-breakfast called Grace Chapel Inn, and they had the privilege of hosting interesting guests from around the world. They had closed the inn for the week, though, and were enjoying having time to be alone with family. "He harvests his own lobsters. Wasn't that a wonderful gift?"

"Yes, it certainly was. You must have really impressed him with the inn's hospitality," Cynthia said.

"He and his wife were on a second honeymoon, and, yes, they were delighted with the inn and with Acorn Hill," her mother told her. "Oh, darling, we're so glad you could make it down for Christmas. We have been counting the days until you arrived."

"I have been too," Cynthia said. "I've been longing for some quiet family time." Cynthia's career of acquiring and editing children's books kept her very busy.

Giving her mother a hug, Cynthia stifled a yawn and laughed. "I guess I'd better turn in. The drive down from Boston wore me out. I'd love to stay up and visit with my three favorite people, but I took the whole week off, so we'll have plenty of time."

Alice and Jane hugged their niece and wished her a good night's sleep.

"Good night darling," Louise said. "I love you."

"Love you too, Mummsy."

Louise smiled. Cynthia hadn't called her that in years.

"I'm not ready for bed," Jane said as Cynthia disappeared upstairs, "but I'd love to get comfy. How about you two? Meet you back here for a cup of hot cider?"

"I'm in," Alice said. "After working all day, my feet are ready for slippers." Alice was a nurse at a local hospital, and though she worked part time, she'd taken a full shift at the hospital so another nurse with children at home could have the day off.

"Sounds like a wonderful idea," Louise said. "Are we finished in the kitchen?"

"All tidy," Jane said. She started up the stairs. "Bet I can beat you both back down."

Alice laughed. "I bet you can too."

When Louise walked back into the kitchen, Jane was wearing a bright red, green, blue and yellow caftan and silver ballet slippers. She was pouring steaming cider into mugs. She plopped a cinnamon stick in each one.

Alice came into the kitchen in her plush blue robe and fuzzy slippers. "Let's have ginger crackles with our cider."

"Good idea," Jane said. They walked into the living room, and Alice pulled their mother's antique rocker closer to the fireplace in the living room. Jane got comfortable on the burgundy sofa. Louise sat on the matching overstuffed chair, resting her feet on an ottoman. She wore a tailored navy robe with white piping and navy mules. Cheery flames danced in the fireplace. Candles flickered on the mantel. The only other illumination came from the colorful lights on the stately Christmas tree. The gold leaf on the faux-painted walls above the wainscoting had a soft sheen.

"This is heavenly," Alice said. "We had a wonderful service tonight, my tummy's full, my toes are warm and I'm sitting here with my favorite sisters."

Jane laughed. "Your only sisters."

Louise took a sip of her cider, then closed her eyes as warmth worked its way through her, inside and out. She tucked her long woolen robe around her legs and gazed at the twinkling Christmas tree lights. "Our tree is beautiful," she said. "Thanks to you, Jane, the decorations seem to get nicer every year. We are so blessed. How many people are so privileged to live in the house they grew up in, in such a lovely town, surrounded by close family?"

"Our lives are idyllic," Jane said. "Do you ever wish you'd moved away, Alice?"

"Never. I know you and Louise have experienced a rich variety of people and places in your lives, but being away for college was enough for me. I've never wanted to live anywhere else."

"I wouldn't trade my years in the city or the traveling we did, but I'm glad we all ended up here where we began—together," Louise said.

"I'd say we had a charmed childhood," Jane said.

"I'd have to agree. At least most of the time."

"Most of the time?" Jane asked.

"Well..." Louise shook her head and smiled. "I don't know why, but our beautiful tree reminds me of the saddest little one I've ever seen."

"Do you mean the year we were at Aunt Ethel's farm for Christmas?" Alice asked.

Louise nodded. "That's the one."

"When was this?" Jane tilted her head. "I don't remember that."

"You weren't even born yet," Louise laughed.

"Well, what happened?" Jane asked, taking a sip of cider.

Louise settled back in her chair. "It was Christmas Eve 1951," she said. "And we'd just shown up at the farm...."

Louise's Christmas Memory

*L*ouise opened the back door of the aging Packard and stepped onto the running board. The ground below her feet was covered with a light dusting of snow, and big fluffy flakes were falling gently in the yard of Aunt Ethel and Uncle Bob's farm. She instinctively stuck her tongue out to catch a frozen crystal, then remembered that she was fourteen, too old for such silliness.

Alice, on the other side of the auto, wasn't worried about looking childish. Three years made a big difference in maturity. Alice chased after flakes, extending her bright red mittens so that snow landed on her palms. Her long reddish-brown braids stuck out on either side of a striped yellow and green stocking cap, and her green wool coat was open, as usual, flapping in the wind.

Louise stepped down to the hard-packed dirt

driveway with exaggerated dignity. Her navy wool coat was securely buttoned all the way to the small collar that hugged her throat, but she hadn't covered her short-cropped reddish hair with a hat so it wouldn't get messed up. Like her sister, she was wearing blue jeans and a warm woolen sweater for this unplanned visit to Aunt Ethel's farm on the day before Christmas.

"Well, girls," her father, Daniel Howard, said in the deep voice that Louise loved to hear when he preached at Grace Chapel in Acorn Hill. "Old Betsy got us here safely this morning, thank the Lord."

Louise said a silent "amen," grateful that they hadn't had a flat tire or engine failure on the way. The prewar car had seen better days. She knew her parents were saving to buy a more reliable, newer auto, but Father said it would take a long time to put away enough on a pastor's salary.

Her father went around to the passenger side and opened the door for her mother Madeleine. He was always courteous, but he was taking special care that her mother didn't fall. She was pregnant, but she hadn't wanted to be left out of this trip to the farm.

"Watch your step," Father said.

"I'm fine," Mother insisted, holding the front of her everyday brown tweed coat closed because it wouldn't button anymore.

Louise watched her mother's face as she held onto her father's arm. Her deep blue eyes looked weary, and there were dark circles under them. In place of her usual sweet smile, her mouth pulled in a straight line.

Aunt Ethel, her father's half-sister, and her husband Bob were supposed to come to Acorn Hill for a Christmas Day celebration with the Howard family. Then Uncle Bob had hurt his back lifting heavy feed sacks. According to Aunt Ethel, he was having terrible spasms. The doctor had recommended that Uncle Bob lie flat for a few days. He was absolutely forbidden to do his farm chores until his back was better.

Father had received an urgent phone call from Aunt Ethel early that morning. One of the farm's ewes was acting up. Aunt Ethel guessed that it was ready to deliver sooner than the rest of the flock, the county's only vet was out of town for the holidays and Aunt Ethel was panicking. She hoped her brother could help.

Alice gave up chasing snowflakes and came up beside the car as Father hauled a brown paper shopping bag from the floor of the back seat, then gave his arm back to Mother.

"Can I carry it?" Alice asked, eagerly taking the bag with gifts for their aunt and uncle.

"I hope the snow stops so we don't have trouble getting home in time for the Christmas Eve service," Mother said, brushing flakes away from her mahogany curls.

"Let's get inside," Father said, guiding her over the uneven ground to the back door of the two-story house that had been in Bob's family for several generations. It was a typical Pennsylvania farm home, with a rough stone foundation and narrow wooden siding. The white paint was nearly worn off. Snow was collecting on the dark shingled roof. A small apple orchard bordered the south side, and the fenced remains of a vegetable garden lay withering on the opposite side. A small wooden windmill on the edge of the cultivated patch, more decorative than practical, was whirling madly as gusts of wind tore across the open ground.

Louise followed reluctantly. She was afraid she might not get back in time for the rehearsal her friends were planning for their Christmas caroling after church that evening. Twelve classmates had practiced with the church choir director several times after school, and they had even saved babysitting money for identical red and green stocking caps. Two of her best friends were in the group, and they'd been talking about caroling for ages.

Alice raced ahead, swinging the bag of gifts while their mother warned her not to let them spill out and ruin the wrappings on the snowy ground.

In spite of herself, Louise had to smile at Father. He was wearing a hat with ear flaps and an oversize khaki coat. His tall, slender form reminded her of a scarecrow, and she could imagine him out in one of the withered fields, arms flapping at the crows who dived down to glean what they could from the remains of last season's crops.

She looked around at the brown and white landscape. This wasn't at all like visiting the farm in the summer, when the fields were patterns of green and the distant hills seemed to sparkle under a hot sun. During a visit last spring, she'd seen baby ducklings on the small pond beyond the barn. She smiled at the memory of the tiny ducklings following their mother in a miniature parade. The only time she loved being here more was in the fall when the trees turned every shade of yellow, orange and red.

She sighed. This wasn't going to be fun the way those visits had been.

The path led to the back door, which Father opened, calling out to announce their arrival. They stepped into the musty-smelling utility room, a long, low space that had been the original cabin when the Buckleys first settled the land. When one of Uncle Bob's ancestors built the family home, he'd attached it to the old building. Now it served as a laundry room and storage space.

Aunt Ethel's wringer-washer sat by a pair of tin tubs on legs. Last summer Louise had helped her aunt fish clothes from the wash water with a broom handle and dunk them into the rinse water in the tubs. It seemed like fun then, but she wouldn't want to have to do that all the time. Lines were strung across part of the room for drying clothes in bad weather. Two pairs of overalls held in place by wooden clothespins hung like stiff cardboard from one line.

Aunt Ethel flung open the door to the main house as they were taking off their snow boots. She rushed out to greet them.

"I can't tell you how glad I am to see you," Aunt Ethel said, stepping aside to let them into the main part of the house. "Bob is hurting so bad, and I don't know what to do when Nellie Belle delivers."

Louise saw that her aunt's small, freckled face looked more pale than usual. Her red hair, normally carefully arranged, was frizzy today. She was dressed in blue jeans and a lime-green wool sweater that had gotten nubby with wear.

In spite of Uncle Bob's objection, Aunt Ethel insisted on naming all their animals. Uncle Bob didn't want her to make pets out of livestock destined for market, but after nearly two years of marriage, he'd given up trying to change her ways.

"Thank you so much for coming," Aunt Ethel said to Father.

"You know we're glad to come when you need us," he said. "We're sorry Bob isn't up to making the trip to Acorn Hill tomorrow, but we'll have our Christmas together this afternoon before we go back."

Alice went into the house to put their gifts under the tree in the parlor. Louise followed her parents into the cozy and old-fashioned kitchen and hung her coat on one of the hooks on the far wall next to an assortment of outdoor clothing.

"How are you feeling, Madeleine?" Aunt Ethel asked. "I'm a little surprised you made the drive here in your condition."

"I'm not so far along that I can't go for a ride," Mother said. "We can't stay long though. Daniel has to preach tonight."

"Of course. I'm sorry to bring you out here, but I'm at my wit's end with Bob laid up."

"How's he doing?" Father asked.

"He's about out of his mind, not being able to get around and do his chores."

"I'll go have a word with him."

"Can I see Uncle Bob too?" Alice asked, coming back into the kitchen with the empty shopping bag.

"I'm not sure you should bother him," Mother said.

"Oh, he would love to see his little princess," Aunt Ethel said. "You go right on up with your Father, Alice."

Louise would have liked to see him too, but when Aunt Ethel said one thing and her mother said another, it seemed best to do as her mother wished. Aunt Ethel was trying to be nice, but she had a habit of contradicting what Mother said.

Alice and Father trooped up the stairs. Mother eased herself onto one of the pressback wooden chairs that surrounded a round oak table covered with a red and black oilcloth. It reminded Louise of a checkerboard. Aunt Ethel had tried to make the old kitchen seem cheerful. She had scattered braided throw rugs over the bare spots on the drab tan lino-leum and painted the walls and the two small wall cupboards a bright yellow. Most of the dishes and kitchenware were stored in two big cabinets that crowded the room, one of them painted a gleaming emerald green. The older one, an antique that had been in Bob's family for generations, still had its natural wood finish, and Louise liked it the best of anything in the room.

"Can I get you something?" her aunt asked, including Louise in her offer. "Maybe some coffee, or I have fresh buttermilk. It's pasteurized from the dairy, so you don't need to worry about it, Madeleine."

"Buttermilk would be nice," Mother said.

"I don't need to ask whether you like buttermilk, do I?" she quipped to Louise.

Her aunt poured the milk into glasses with fan-ciful bears on them, the kind you got free for saving food labels, then put a big tomato-red Fiestaware plate of Christmas cookies on the table. There were trees, Santas, stars and even rabbits covered with red and green frosting and bright-colored sugars.

"Is that coffee I smell?" Father asked, coming back into the kitchen with Alice on his heels. "I could use a cup to warm up before we go out to the barn."

While her father sipped his coffee, Louise helped herself to a red-frosted rabbit, idly wondering why Aunt Ethel had chosen an Easter cookie cutter. She took two bites and decided it was too sweet. Her sharp-eyed aunt noticed when she started breaking the cookie into pieces instead of eating it.

"You won't hurt my feelings if you don't like it," Aunt Ethel said. "My neighbor made the cookies. She brought them over when she heard Bob was hurt. It was nice of her, of course, but she overdoes everything from cookies to kids. She has seven children, and she's on her second husband—"

"Ethel, I'm teaching the girls not to listen to gossip or pass it on," Mother interrupted gently.

"I just—" Aunt Ethel began, her face turning red.

"You know, I really should see that ewe of yours," Father said quickly. "Bob is worried because it's her first lambing. Who wants to go out to the barn with me?"

"If Ethel doesn't mind, I think I'll rest in the parlor for a few minutes," Mother said.

"Well no, of course I don't mind. One of Grandma Buckley's afghans is on the back of the davenport if you want to lie down. Let me know if you need another cover. Are you sure you're okay?"

"Thank you, Ethel. I'm just a little tired."

"Her back has been keeping her awake at night," Father explained. "I'm afraid the car ride made it worse."

"Nonsense," Mother said. "It did me good to get out. I've never enjoyed just sitting around the house."

"Who's coming with me?" Father asked.

"I am!" Alice called. Her footsteps thunked on the wooden steps. "I want to see the sheep and the barn kitties."

"I'll come too," Louise said.

They trooped out to the utility room to find their boots, and by the time Louise had buckled hers, Aunt Ethel was ready to lead them out to the barn. She looked a bit like a scarecrow too, wearing a thick brown cable-knit cardigan instead of a coat, her thin legs thrust into three-buckle black boots. But she was too cheerful for a scarecrow, with her flaming red hair and smiling face.

As soon as she stepped outside, a fierce wind whipped about them. The fluffy flakes were no longer falling, but the slate-gray sky hinted that there was more snow to come. Aunt Ethel hugged the sweater around her and trotted toward the barn with Father at her side. Alice had raced ahead, and Louise brought up the rear.

The barn looked very old to Louise. It had a stone foundation higher than her head, and the planks on the upper part were a faded white.

Her aunt urged her to hurry inside, then slammed the big barn door behind her. The barn smelled of hay bales and confined animals, which bothered Louise, but Alice didn't seem to notice. She quickly climbed into one of the pens and was petting a big sheep with grayish-white wool.

Louise looked around the barn. The floor was divided into several pens, including one with a lone sheep.

"This is Nellie Belle in the lambing pen," Aunt Ethel said. "Oh, I know your uncle doesn't like me to name animals, but what should I do, call them Sheep one and Sheep two?"

"Father calls our car Betsy. Isn't that silly?" Alice said with a giggle.

"Maybe naming things runs in the family," he said, reaching out and tugging on one of Alice's braids.

Louise didn't know much about sheep, but she understood the sorrowful moaning of the poor ewe in the pen. Her eyes got teary. "She sounds so sad," she said.

Father stepped into the pen and stooped beside the ewe. She was one of the smaller ones, with thick white wool that looked dingy in the subdued light filtering in from the small, high window at the front of the barn.

"Can you give me more light?" he asked.

"I'll light a lantern," Aunt Ethel said. "Bob says it's too expensive to run electricity to the barn. The old kerosene stove that we use to keep the newborns warm makes me nervous, but at least Bob has it sitting on a slab of cement."

Alice had run to the back of the barn to see whether she could coax any of the barn cats to come play with her, but they were not a friendly bunch and remained in hiding. Alice came back and hung on the fencing that marked off the lambing pen.

Her father stood and looked at Louise, who was standing frozen in place just outside the fenced area.

"It sounds like she's crying," Louise said.

"She may be a little frightened," he said, "but I'm sure everything will be fine. Why don't you take Alice back to the house? I think Aunt Ethel has some board games you can play."

"Yes, they're in the window seat in the parlor. Just be really quiet so you don't wake your mother if she's sleeping," her aunt warned.

"Oh, Father, I want to stay here. Please let me stay," Alice begged.

"I'm not sure you should," he said in a hesitant voice.

"Please, pretty please, with sugar on top."

Father shook his head but didn't insist that Alice leave.

"I'm going back to the house. Maybe Mommy is awake and wants company," Louise said. Plus, she might be able to convince her mother to let them start back to town sooner rather than later.

"Always my sensitive girl," Louise heard her father say as she stepped out into the worsening weather.

When Louise came into the parlor, her mother was sitting on the davenport with a crocheted afghan tucked around her. Her face was pale in contrast to the bright-colored squares bordered in black. She wore a sad expression that wasn't at all like her.

"Are you all right?" Louise asked, sitting down beside her.

"Yes, of course. I was just thinking."

"About?" Louise asked.

"I'm worried that your father takes on too much. I know he wanted to use today to polish his sermon and to make sure everything was ready for this evening's service. His congregation expects so much from him. So does your aunt."

Louise had come to realize that a pastor's family had to adjust their lives around his schedule. Father sometimes worked long hours and was called out in the middle of the night when a member of the congregation needed him. A lot was expected of a minister's wife, too, and Mother worked hard for the church. And Louise understood that there were expectations for preachers' kids as well. If she or Alice behaved badly, it reflected on their father.

"Maybe you should have stayed home," Louise said sympathetically. "I would have stayed with you."

"It's the day before Christmas. It's a time for family to be together." Her mother smiled and gave Louise a hug. "How is the ewe?" she asked. "Does your father think it will be long before the lamb comes?"

"He didn't say. The mother seemed to be suffering a lot. I felt so sorry for her. Do you think she'll be all right?"

"I expect so. Most sheep don't have much trouble giving birth—at least that's what your uncle Bob said once. He should know."

"Is Uncle Bob going to be all right? I hate it that everything is going wrong at Christmastime."

"Not everything," her mother said, stroking her hand. "We have a wonderful family. Your father loves preaching the Word of the Lord, and he loves all of us very much. And think about it, we get to have Christmas twice, once here and again at home."

"It doesn't feel right, not being home getting ready for Christmas Eve. I still have a special present to wrap, and I promised Alice I'd help her make a paper chain to decorate the mantel like we always do. We were going to make a batch of peanut brittle this afternoon, and we haven't hung our socks. And I have to be back in time to get ready for caroling."

"I'm sorry, dear, but think how lonely it would be for your father if he had to drive here and back alone."

Louise knew her mother was right, but it didn't make her feel any happier. The sky visible through the parlor window matched her mood: dark and gloomy. What if the weather prevented them from leaving? She couldn't imagine missing the Christmas Eve service and the caroling.

A door slammed.

"It shouldn't be long now," Aunt Ethel said, coming into the parlor a moment later. "Madeleine, I can't tell you how much I appreciate Daniel's help. I've had nightmares about all the ewes lambing at once with no one to help me. I know it relieved Bob's mind, too, that you came. I'm hoping he can make it downstairs for the present exchange. Christmas is really important in his family. My mother-in-law has told me about all kinds of German customs that they observe in Bob's family. This is only our second

Christmas as a married couple. Somehow that makes it even worse that he's laid up."

Amazingly, Aunt Ethel had managed to say all that without taking a breath. The wind had tangled her hair into a wild halo and colored her cheeks bright red. Her presence lightened Louise's mood.

"How long do you think the lambing will take?" her mother asked.

Aunt Ethel shrugged and shook her head. "I wish I knew. It's Nellie Belle's first—maybe I told you that already."

"You did."

"Is Father going to let Alice help?" Louise asked.

"I'm not sure 'let' is the right word," her aunt said with a light laugh. "She's bound and determined to be there when the lamb arrives."

"That's my Alice," Mother said with a warm smile. "I've never known a child who loves all God's creatures as much as she does—not that Louise isn't kind and caring with animals. I depend on her to feed our cat and keep her water dish fresh."

Louise knew that her mother never complimented one of them without saying something nice about the other, but Alice got full credit for being the animal lover.

"If things go wrong with the lamb...," Aunt Ethel said.

"Don't worry. Daniel will send Alice back to the house if he thinks it's too much for her."

Did her mother mean that the lamb might not be okay? Or that the ewe might die giving birth? Louise felt a twinge of fear, and she wished that her mother was home safe without the worry of a lambing that could go wrong.

"Can I get you anything to eat or drink?" Aunt Ethel asked the two of them.

"Not now, thank you," Mother said. "I'll wait until Daniel can eat."

Louise looked around the room. The parlor was crowded with too much furniture, most of it old, things left when Uncle Bob's parents retired and moved out of the farmhouse. Ethel had an astonishing number of framed pictures and knickknacks displayed on every surface in the room. Louise tried the old upright piano every time she visited, but taking care of it wasn't a priority for her aunt and uncle, and it was badly out of tune.

She walked over to the Christmas tree. She thought it was the saddest tree she'd ever seen. Its limbs were widely spaced, and garlands of popcorn and cranberries only emphasized how many needles had already fallen.

"I know it's not much of a tree. I needed to pick something small because I had to handle it myself, and I cut it much too early," Aunt Ethel said. "Bob's family never puts up theirs until Christmas Eve. That's the German tradition, but I couldn't wait to decorate ours. Unfortunately the lights and glass ornaments are packed away somewhere in the attic. Since Bob got hurt, I'm sort of scared to go up there alone."

"You did a good job stringing popcorn," Louise said, wanting to say something nice about the scrawny tree.

"There's not much else to do here in the evening, especially since Bob has to lie flat all the time." Aunt Ethel said this matter-of-factly.

An awkward silence stretched out.

"I have an idea," Aunt Ethel said. "I was going to make some *frobelsterne*, German paper stars. I have the construction paper, but I never got around to it with having to take care of Bob and the animals. Maybe you could help me."

"I don't know how," Louise said.

"Oh, a clever girl like you will catch on right away. It's all in how you fold them," her aunt assured her.

"It sounds like fun," Mother said.

"I'll get the paper. We can work in the kitchen," Aunt Ethel said.

They gathered around the table and stripped the oilcloth off so they wouldn't damage it as they cut sheets of construction paper into the right sizes to fold.

"Someday I want a new table, one with shiny chrome legs," Aunt Ethel said, looking at the scratched and stained surface of the table. "For now, though, improvements on the farm come first. Bob thinks we need to have a new well drilled in the spring, and that barn is crying out for a coat of whitewash. I'm learning that the house comes last when you're trying to make a go of farming."

"Show us how to make stars," Madeleine prompted her. "What did you call them?"

"Frobelsterne. What color would you like, Louise? I have white, blue and yellow construction paper."

She reached for a sheet of blue, her favorite color, and picked up a pair of scissors.

Aunt Ethel demonstrated how to cut the paper

to the right size and fold it into a three-dimensional star, using a short length of wire from a spool to make a hanger. Her mother quickly completed a white star, but Louise felt all thumbs. She tried to concentrate on what she was doing, but she was thinking about what was happening in the barn. What if the lamb didn't come? How long would they stay? If she knew her father, he would hate leaving before he knew that the lamb had arrived safely.

"I can't stop thinking about the ewe. She seemed so unhappy," Louise said.

"She'll be okay," Mother said. "It's wonderful when new life comes into the world. It's the greatest gift of all from our Lord."

Her mother's words made her feel better, but Louise was still worried that the lamb would take so long to come that they wouldn't get home in time for all the wonderful things they did to celebrate Christmas Eve. Even worse, if the lamb didn't survive, Alice would be miserable. It would be terrible for her little sister if something bad happened with the lamb or the ewe.

Her mother stood and rubbed her back before starting to work on another star. Louise had a really scary thought. Would her mother suffer the way the ewe was suffering when it came time for the new baby to come?

"Why don't you start over with new paper?" Aunt Ethel kindly suggested when Louise held up a misshapen blob that barely resembled a star. "Here, I'll fold one, and you can imitate what I do."

Her mother sat down to fold another frobel-sterne, and Louise tried to give her full attention to making a pretty one of her own.

"Splendid!" Aunt Ethel said when she finally made a fairly decent star.

They worked quietly for nearly half an hour, but all three of them watched the entrance to the kitchen, hoping for good news from the barn.

"I didn't think it would take Nellie Belle this long," Aunt Ethel said.

"She's in good hands with Daniel," Mother comforted her. "I'm sure he's praying for a successful delivery. He loves animals. I guess that's where Alice gets it."

Louise offered a silent prayer that all was well with the ewe.

The stars piled up, and they agreed to wait so

that Alice could help hang them later. Ethel left the table to baste the two chickens that she had in the oven for their midday dinner.

"I don't want to send you folks home hungry," she said. "I wasn't much of a cook when we got married, but I'm learning, slowly but surely."

"I'm sure it will be a lovely meal," Mother said.

Louise could detect the wistfulness in her voice. Christmas Eve Day was always a special time for their family, and she knew her mother was as eager to get home as she was. It had started snowing again. They would need to leave soon in order to get home safely through the storm. Louise said another silent prayer for the ewe to deliver successfully, and soon.

The outer door of the utility room blew shut with so much force that Louise could feel the floor shake under her feet. Seconds later, Alice ran into the room.

"Alice, your boots," her mother automatically reminded her.

She looked down, as though surprised that she

was wearing them, and Aunt Ethel leaped to her defense.

"It doesn't matter a bit on this old floor. How is Nellie Belle? Is the lamb here?"

"No, not yet," Alice said with a worried frown. "Father wants to stay with her, but he told me to come here. He doesn't think it will be long now."

"Well, you're just in time to help make some frobelsterne," Aunt Ethel said with exaggerated enthusiasm. "See what pretty ones your mother and sister have made. What color would you like to try?"

She dangled a star in front of Alice.

"None, thank you. Father might need me. I'd better go back to the barn."

"If your father sent you here, it means he doesn't think it's a good idea for you to be there," Mother said. "Now be a good girl and take off your boots and coat."

Alice usually did what she was told, but being kept away from animals brought out her stubborn side. Mother would be upset if Alice was naughty, and that was the last thing Louise wanted.

"I've made enough stars," Louise quickly said. "I'll go outside with you, Alice. Maybe we can build a snowman or something."

"That's a good idea," Mother said, "but you'd better put something on your head, Louise. I don't want you getting a cold for the holidays."

Louise started to protest, but Aunt Ethel was too quick for her.

"I have just what you need," she said, darting over to the shelf above the coat hooks and bringing down a wad of yellowish-green wool. "My mother-in-law made this for me, but I hardly ever remember to wear it."

Louise took the knitted hat and thought no one but a really old woman would wear a bonnet with strings that tied under the chin.

"I don't need it," she protested.

"Please wear it without a fuss," her mother said.

She plopped it on her head and loosely knotted the ties, glad that none of her friends would see her wearing such a monstrosity. Alice went back outside while Louise put on her coat and mittens.

"I think it's best that Alice doesn't go back to the barn until your father calls her," Mother said.

"How can I stop her?" Louise asked, rather dismayed at the prospect of keeping her sister occupied and away from the ewe.

"Please, just play with her for a bit. I would really appreciate it."

Her mother smiled, leaving Louise with no choice but to do her best. Alice wasn't going to be enthusiastic about making a snowman when she was on pins and needles about the lambing.

When she got outside, Alice was shuffling through the snow where it had drifted against the side of the house, trying her best to find spots that were over her boots.

"What do you want to do?" Louise asked.

"Go back to the barn."

"Not until Father calls you. Mother said so."

"I want to help with the lamb."

"You can go there when he calls," she repeated less patiently.

She and Alice used to play together all the time, but lately they weren't interested in the same things.

"Let's make a snowman," Louise suggested. "I bet it would look funny wearing this awful hat of Aunt Ethel's."

"It's not good packing," her sister argued.

Louise ran over to a large patch of lawn that had a good snow covering and grabbed a big handful.

"Let's see who can make the biggest snowball," she challenged her sister.

Unfortunately, Alice was right. The snow fell apart in their hands.

"I told you it wasn't good packing," Alice said with a halfhearted attempt to throw her snowball at Louise.

"I have a better idea." Louise stared at the windswept snow. "Let's make snow angels to watch over Nellie Belle."

She led the way by flopping down on her back, fanning out her arms to make the outline of wings in the snow.

After a moment's hesitation, Alice dropped down a few yards away and energetically moved her arms up and down by her sides.

Louise could feel cold snow creeping between her boots and jeans, and her coat collar didn't keep her neck dry. Wind was lashing at her face, and her hair was going to be a sight when she went to the Christmas Eve service. Unless they left soon, there wouldn't be time to wash it and get it dry. She wondered whether it was right to pray that a lamb hurry up and be born.

Alice was making two angels for every one

Louise finished. The way the wind was blowing, they would soon be erased, but for now, they were both having fun.

She'd just stood up after making her third angel when she heard a voice over the din of the wind.

"Alice, Louise, tell your aunt that the lamb is here, then come see it."

Alice nearly fell down in her hurry to get to the barn. Louise opened the door to the utility room and called to her aunt and mother, "The lamb's here!" Then she turned and caught up with Alice, thanking the Lord that now they could go home soon.

Her father opened the door just wide enough for them to squeeze through, quickly shutting it to keep out the frigid wind.

Alice danced around the outside of the birthing pen, where Daniel had covered the lamb with an old blue towel to keep it warm.

"It's so beautiful," Alice said, awestruck by the tiny creature.

"It's a girl," Father said with a smile. "I lit the kerosene stove so she wouldn't get cold."

Louise was amazed as she looked at the tiny head and dainty little hooves sticking out from the worn towel. The lamb was easily the most beautiful thing she'd ever seen.

"How did it go?" Aunt Ethel asked, squeezing in between the door and the frame.

"Not too badly," Father said. "She nursed a little."

"That's good," his sister said. "Newborn lambs must get colostrum from the ewe. Without it, they're vulnerable to diseases like pneumonia. It's always a worry that a lamb won't nurse."

"I don't think we're over the hump yet," Father said, looking at Alice's expectant face. "The lamb is pretty weak. She's going to need supplemental feeding."

"I'm prepared for that. I have a tiny bottle, and I can get goat's milk from a neighbor," Aunt Ethel said. "Mr. Seifert has a large flock of goats. He offered the milk because it's the best supplement for a lamb if the mother doesn't have enough milk."

"So it's going to be okay?" Alice's face lit up.

"Daniel, I can't thank you enough for what you've done, but you will stay to open presents, won't you? I have chicken in the oven for dinner. Can't let you drive home with empty tummies."

"Can I feed the lamb?" Alice asked.

"We'll see," her father said.

Alice clung to the side of the pen, reluctant to leave. Louise felt the same way. The tiny white face looked so vulnerable, and her wooly mother didn't seem very interested in her.

"We can come back when your aunt gets the goat milk," Father promised.

They trudged back to the house through swirling snow.

"I can see by your faces that you have good news," Mother said when they were hanging up their damp coats.

"Yes, the lamb took a little colostrum from the ewe," Ethel said, "but I'm worried that she isn't going to be a good mother. I'm going down the road to get some goat's milk from a neighbor. Lambs have to have nourishment immediately after birth if they're going to survive."

"I'll drive you," Father offered.

"Thank you, Daniel. I'll make some hot chocolate when we get back. It will only take us a few minutes," Aunt Ethel said.

"Why don't I make it while you're gone," Mother offered. "Just show me where the cocoa powder and sugar are."

"I can handle it when I get back," Ethel said. "You may not know where things are."

Mother watched her for a moment and then took in a deep breath. "Okay," she said quietly.

"No going to the barn until I get back," Father warned Alice.

"Can I go up and see Uncle Bob?" Louise asked.

"Not now, honey," Aunt Ethel said. "He's taking a nap, but there's good news. He's going to come downstairs to open gifts. It helped his back a lot to lie still, although it must be really tedious, doing nothing but listening to his radio."

"Can I listen to Edgar Bergen and Charlie McCarthy?" Alice asked.

"I doubt it's on tonight."

"But if it is?" Alice wasn't easily discouraged.

"We have too much else planned for Christmas Eve. When we get home, we'll have to hurry to get ready for church."

Alice nodded, but Louise wasn't sure she really understood.

"I hope Father gets back soon," Alice said. Father and Aunt Ethel hadn't been gone long, but they didn't have far to travel.

"If you like, you can put on your coat and boots and wait for him in the utility room," Mother said. "But don't go outside until they're back."

Alice took her coat from the hook and struggled into it on the way to the back room.

"I know how she feels," Mother said with a sigh. "I'm as impatient to start back as she is to see the lamb."

Louise heartily agreed. The quicker they ate and opened presents, the sooner they could leave for home. She was still hopeful she wouldn't have to miss any of the things she loved about Christmas Eve. It was her favorite service of the year. Father and Aunt Ethel seemed to be gone for ages.

"They probably had to wait for the goat to be milked," Mother suggested.

"But it's taking them forever," Louise said.

"They're not back yet," Alice said, poking her head into the kitchen. "What's taking them so long? Can't I go see the lamb?"

"Wait for your father," her mother said. "Time always seems to go slowly when you're impatient."

Alice went back to her vigil, and Mother smiled at Louise.

"It's hard to wait," she said, "especially for Alice. When she was little, she drove us crazy wanting to open her presents early. We had to hide them. You were just the opposite. You loved looking at packages and imagining what was in them. I think you would have saved them until July if your father hadn't urged you to open them."

Louise wasn't excited about gifts this year. She only wanted to go home so they wouldn't miss any of the Christmas Eve celebration at church. She thought of last year's service. Everyone held little candles with paper around them to catch the drips. As the service ended, the ushers lit one person's candle at the end of each pew, and the flame was passed down the rows. The electric lights were extinguished, and the congregation sang "Silent Night" in the glow of candlelight. She'd had to fight back tears because it was so beautiful. If only her father would return so they could go home.

When Father finally did come, he was alone.

"Ethel and Alice went to feed the lamb," he explained. He didn't even take off his coat before sitting down at the table. "I'm afraid I have bad news."

"It's the weather, isn't it?" Mother asked. "Even without going outside, I can tell it's getting worse."

"It's snowing harder, and I'm worried about the roads. There's drifting in places, and it took quite some time just to go a mile to get the goat's milk."

"We should leave right now then," Mother said. "I know Ethel will be disappointed, but we don't have time for dinner and presents."

"Actually," he said, clearing his throat the way he did when he had something unpleasant to say, "I think I'd better go back to Acorn Hill alone."

"But we have to go with you!" Louise blurted out. "It's Christmas Eve."

"I know you want to, honey, but the storm is getting worse. I think you girls and your mother should stay here overnight. I'll come get you as soon as I can tomorrow."

"I can't miss the Christmas Eve service," Louise argued. "If the roads are safe enough for you, they're safe enough for me—for all of us."

"If the car should go off the road and get stuck, I can hike to the nearest farm and get help, but it's too cold to leave all of you in the car. And Louise, you know your mother can't be out walking in the middle of a snow storm in her condition."

"If the weather is as bad as you say, maybe no one will show up for the evening service," Mother said. "You could stay here with us."

Father spoke softly but firmly, looking as unhappy as Louise felt. "People in town will get there, and I should be there for the service."

"We should all be together as a family on Christmas Eve," Mother said. There was an edge to her voice.

"I wish we could be, but I can't put you in danger," Daniel insisted. "You'll be safe on the farm. Ethel and Bob will be delighted to have you overnight. They're facing a lonely Christmas Eve with Bob laid up, and Ethel will have her hands full taking care of the lamb through the night. The first twenty-four hours are the crucial time for a newborn lamb."

"And spending holidays with your wife and children are crucial to a family." Mother's jaw was set, and her shoulders were hunched up.

"The people at church don't need you as much as we do," Louise said, feeling close to tears.

"Someone will read your sermon for you if you

can't get back," Mother insisted. Louise was old enough to see that sometimes her mother got frustrated by how much time Father spent away from his family in church meetings. "What if only one person shows up for church? Is it worth risking the drive back in a storm?"

"I don't like this either," Father said. "I don't want to be away from you on Christmas Eve. But remember the parable of the lost sheep," he said in a regretful voice. "Even though ninety-nine members of the flock were safe, the shepherd searched for the one who was lost. If one person shows up, I'm still responsible for being there. It's my calling, but I need your help. I have to know you're safe before I set out in this weather."

"I wish you wouldn't go," Mother said, but her voice told Louise that she was wavering.

Daniel leaned over her and tenderly kissed her cheek. "You know how much I'll miss you, but I can't risk taking you and the girls out in a storm."

"Our car is so old. I don't trust it anymore," Mother said.

"Old Betsy will get me to Acorn Hill and back here tomorrow. It's not her first storm," he said, attempting to lighten the mood. "I'll get you home for Christmas Day."

They said their good-byes, and Father assured Mother that he'd call their guests for this evening and tell them that dinner was canceled. Then her father asked Louise to come to the utility room with him while he put on his boots.

All Louise could think was that this was just like her tenth birthday party. She had counted on her father to be there, but something had kept him at church until it was all over. It wasn't always easy to be the pastor's daughter. Family plans had to be put on hold whenever a sick or grieving member needed him.

"I know you're disappointed," he said. "I would take you with me, but I need you here to look after your mother. She's not as strong as she seems. You can help her with Alice. Aunt Ethel may have to stay up all night with the lamb. It's very fragile. Lambs can be lost if they don't feed well right away, but Alice should go to bed at a reasonable time."

"Do you think the lamb will die?" Louise asked in alarm.

"No, I'm hopeful that it won't, but just in case,

I need you to be strong for your sister and your mother. And your aunt too."

"I don't want you to go, Father." Louise tried to be brave, but her voice shook.

"I'll be fine." He tousled her hair as though she were still his little girl and kissed her forehead. "Take care of your mother. I'll be back."

Louise stood at the open door watching him tramp through snowdrifts with a fierce wind in his face. The snow angels had already been swept away by the storm, and she was sad to see them gone.

She couldn't believe they would miss the family's special Christmas Eve celebration. They always had supper after the service, sometimes inviting a select group of friends. Then they would gather around the piano and sing their favorite Christmas songs. After the guests left and Alice went to bed, Louise would help her parents fill their Christmas stockings. It was precious time alone with both her mother and father. It just wasn't fair that she had to miss it this year.

She was letting cold air into the already frigid utility room, but she couldn't make herself look away until her father was in the car and slowly driving out to the road. She didn't shut the door until the bulky old vehicle was only a blur.

"Dear Lord," she prayed, "please let Father get home safely, and help me not to be angry because I've been left behind."

She brushed away a tear and watched as Alice and her aunt pushed through the snow toward the house.

"And please, Lord, let the baby lamb live. It would break Alice's heart to lose it."

∽

They never did have hot chocolate, but following the tradition of farm families, Aunt Ethel had planned the midday meal to be the biggest of the day. After Daniel left, she had put out her colorful Fiestaware plates—tomato red, cobalt blue, aqua and yellow—and started to bring the food to the table.

Louise helped to set the table while Alice moped around, worried that she should be in the barn with the lamb. Mother offered to help with the meal, but Aunt Ethel insisted she rest and just watch while Ethel tackled the job of carving the stuffed chickens.

"I'll take a tray up to your uncle Bob, then we can eat," her aunt said. She carefully arranged the wooden tray she'd covered with a yellow linen cloth, choosing the cobalt-blue plate from her multicolored set for her husband's dinner. The place setting was pretty, but Louise wasn't so sure about the food. The chicken leg crackled loudly when Ethel carved it off, and the mashed potatoes spread across the plate in a mushy blob. Poor Aunt Ethel wasn't known for her cooking, and the lamb had occupied her thoughts and delayed the meal, which hadn't helped things.

"Who would like to say the blessing?" Aunt Ethel asked when they were seated around the table.

"Me," Alice volunteered.

"That would be nice," her aunt said.

"God is good, God is great, let us thank Him for our food. Amen," Alice said, reaching for a bowl of canned applesauce as soon as she concluded.

"That was a good prayer, Alice." Aunt Ethel picked up her fork.

"You didn't ask the Lord to see Father home safely," Louise said. "You didn't pray that Uncle Bob gets better or that the lamb is okay."

"I said a dinner prayer," Alice said in a hurt voice.

"Prayers should come from the heart," Louise said, quoting something her father often said.

"Girls, please," their mother said. "We're all sad that Father isn't with us. Why don't we have a minute of silent prayer? We can each speak to the Lord about what's closest to our hearts."

Aunt Ethel shot Mother a look.

Louise bowed her head and fervently prayed her father would get home safely through the storm and her mother would be well. She asked that Uncle Bob be healed and that Aunt Ethel be able to manage on her own until his back was better. She also asked forgiveness for being critical of Alice.

"Well, shall we eat?" Aunt Ethel asked. She had already scooped up some potatoes with her fork.

Louise discovered she was hungry enough to eat her serving of white meat after she had pulled off the skin, and the dressing was quite tasty.

But Aunt Ethel couldn't seem to sit still. She kept jumping up to get things they didn't need, and twice in the course of the meal she dashed upstairs to see if her husband needed anything, returning the second time with the tray.

"Uncle Bob hasn't had much appetite since he hurt his back."

She put the tray on the crowded counter and turned a tearful face toward them.

"Sometimes I don't think I'll ever get used to being a farm wife. I try, but bad things just keep happening. Now if something happens to Daniel driving on bad roads, it will be my fault."

There was an awkward moment of silence. Louise didn't know what to do. Then Mother rose and hugged Ethel. "Daniel makes his own decisions. You don't need to blame yourself for anything," she said. Louise could tell she was trying to make Aunt Ethel feel better, but she wasn't sure if Mother actually believed what she was saying. "He'll call us when he gets home. Maybe it won't be storming as much when he gets closer to Acorn Hill."

Mother tried to sound optimistic, but she'd barely touched her food, and worry lines creased her forehead.

"Of course he'll be fine," Aunt Ethel said, wiping away a tear from her cheek. "I'm just being silly. Daniel is a good driver, one of the best. And think how much practice he's had going to visit members of his congregation."

"Yes, he's always comfortable behind the wheel. I just wish I'd gone with him," Mother said. "It's much harder waiting for news than it would have been risking the storm."

Louise wholeheartedly agreed. She remembered Father had told her to look after her mother, so she tried to think of something to say to console her. "I think God wants him to lead the Christmas Eve service. He'll see that Father gets to Grace Chapel safely," she said.

For a moment there was absolute silence in the kitchen, then Mother stepped behind Louise's chair and gave her a big hug.

"You have such strong faith," she said in a husky voice. "Never lose it, no matter what happens in your life."

"Well, will you help me clear the table, Alice?" Aunt Ethel said after a few moments of silence. "I have a bowl of red Jell-O with canned peaches. We can have it for dessert, and I have some of my neighbor's cookies left."

Only Alice wanted Jell-O, so Louise helped with the cleanup while her sister had a big bowl of the wiggly dessert.

"Why don't you have a little rest in the spare bedroom, Madeleine?" Aunt Ethel suggested. "The girls and I will think of something to do. Hey, I know! We can put lights on the Christmas tree."

Louise didn't think a hundred lights would improve the sad little tree, but it was a good idea for her mother to take a nap. In the last month, she'd frequently rested in the afternoon.

"I'll help you carry them down from the attic, Aunt Ethel," she said.

"Me too," Alice said, quickly downing the last spoonful of Jell-O. "Then can we go see the lamb again?"

"Yes, of course. I'll have to keep checking on her, maybe all night. This is the crucial time for a newborn—"

"I think I'll take you up on your offer," Madeleine interrupted with a smile.

Louise guessed that her mother didn't want Alice to worry about the lamb, but she wondered if such a fragile little thing could survive. Her sister was going to be heartbroken if it didn't. Could this Christmas Eve get any worse?

While their mother went upstairs to rest, Aunt

Ethel put the last of the dinner dishes in a rack to dry and dumped the dishpan of water down the sink drain.

"Well, shall we tackle the attic, girls?" she asked as she dried her hands on a flour sack dishtowel.

The three of them tiptoed up the stairs to the second floor, being as quiet as they could so they didn't wake Mother or Uncle Bob if they were sleeping. A door at the end of the corridor opened onto the steps to the attic, and Aunt Ethel led the way, cautioning them to be especially careful going up.

"This is spooky," Alice whispered back to Louise, who came up behind her.

Louise didn't know about spooky, but this was the narrowest staircase she'd ever seen. There were things piled on the lower steps, so there was barely enough room for her feet.

"I hate going up here," Aunt Ethel confided. "That's why I put things on the steps, hoping your uncle Bob will carry them up." She pushed aside a box that seemed to be full of old jelly glasses and went the rest of the way up the dimly lit stairs.

A single bulb lit the area with only a pathway

between stacks of discarded furniture, corrugated cardboard boxes and assorted castoffs. A woman's dress dummy seemed to stand guard over the accumulation, and a large trunk with a domed lid blocked the way to the far end.

"Now where did I put those lights last year?" she mused.

"What's in here?" Alice asked, attempting to lift the heavy lid of the trunk.

"I really don't know," Aunt Ethel said. "Most of this was here when we moved in. My in-laws have a smaller place now and don't have room for any of this. They said to keep whatever we want and discard the rest, but cleaning the attic isn't at the top of Uncle Bob's list."

Alice managed to open the trunk but turned away quickly. "It's a bunch of old paper," she said, letting the top fall shut.

"My boxes are over here," Ethel said. "I've been meaning to go through them, but this place keeps me so busy."

She went over to a cluster of cartons and got down on her knees to look through them. The attic was frigid, and Louise wrapped her arms around herself.

In the attic, the noise of the wind whipping around the house was louder than ever, and Louise shivered, thinking of her father out in the storm.

"Oh, look," Aunt Ethel said with a squeal of pleasure. "Here's the scrapbook I made with our wedding pictures and souvenirs of our honeymoon. We went to a lovely hotel in Maryland. One day we ordered a room-service breakfast. The plates were covered by silver domes to keep the food warm."

"Is that your wedding picture?" Louise asked, bending over to see better.

"Yes. My dress was genuine silk with a really full skirt. My veil was Belgian lace that Bob's uncle brought back from the war. It made me feel like a princess. They're both here somewhere, packed in blue tissue paper to keep them nice. I like to think that someday a daughter of mine will wear them."

"Look, there we are in the picture," Alice said excitedly. "I remember Mother making our dresses."

"I loved the pale green taffeta," Louise said. "That was the first time I wore nylon stockings and shoes with sort-of high heels."

"Oh, look at this," Aunt Ethel exclaimed. "I saved a menu from the hotel dining room. I think I'll take the scrapbook downstairs so it won't get musty. I don't know what I was thinking, leaving it up here."

Alice wandered off, trying to see what else was hidden away in the attic, and managed to bump her head on one of the low rafters.

"Ouch!" she said, rubbing the top of her head.

"Are you all right?" Aunt Ethel asked with a trace of panic in her voice.

"I'm fine. I can hardly feel it now," Alice assured her. "And I found the Christmas lights."

Aunt Ethel went down the attic's stairs first, carrying the box of lights, followed by Alice, who kept her hands on the walls of the staircase because there wasn't a banister. Louise followed carefully with the scrapbook clutched against her.

"Well, that was fun, wasn't it?" Aunt Ethel said when they were back in the parlor. "I'm so glad I found my wedding scrapbook. Would you girls like to look at it while I go down to the cellar and put some coal in the furnace? Or you can come with me, if you like."

"We'll look at the scrapbook," Louise said. The last thing she wanted to do was go down to the basement with its low ceiling, dirt floor and strong earthy odor. This trip to the farm was making her appreciate the lovely old Victorian house where their family lived in comfort. Louise didn't envy the life Aunt Ethel had here.

"Look at this picture of us at the wedding," Alice said with delight. "I can't believe how short I was then."

Louise sat down beside her sister on the davenport. It was fun to look back at the wedding and remember what a good time they'd had. For a few minutes, she forgot how sorry she was to be stuck at the farm on Christmas Eve.

Louise looked up from the scrapbook when she heard her mother coming downstairs.

"Couldn't you sleep, Mother?" she asked.

"I rested a little, but I kept thinking about your father out in the storm. I know he's a good driver, and the Lord will look after him, but I do wish he were here."

"Do you want to look at Aunt Ethel's wedding pictures with us?" Alice asked, making room for her on the davenport.

"Maybe later, dear. I think I'll make myself some tea if your aunt doesn't mind."

"I wouldn't mind at all," Aunt Ethel said, coming into the parlor after her trip to the cellar. "But I'm afraid I don't have any. Bob only drinks coffee, so that's all I have."

"It doesn't matter," Madeleine said. "I was just looking for something to do."

"We're going to put lights on the Christmas tree," Louise said.

"Yes, we helped bring them down from the attic," Alice added.

"That's nice, but Aunt Ethel probably wants to test them first. I never quite trust old strings of lights."

"We bought them last year for our first Christmas together," Ethel said, sounding a bit hurt. "They work fine. The girls can put the frobelsterne on the tree while I untangle the lights."

Alice sat on the worn parlor carpet and played with the stars, arranging them in patterns, then mixing them up again while Louise helped with the lights.

"Is your phone working?" Mother asked Aunt Ethel.

"Of course." Aunt Ethel sniffed.

"Would you mind if I just went to check?" Mother said. "It would relieve my mind to know that Daniel can get through to us when he arrives home."

"I'll do it."

Aunt Ethel returned from the kitchen after a minute or so, a frown making her face look older.

"It's working," she said, "but it's a party line. One of the people on the line is always hogging it, and sure enough, she's chattering away as if she were the only one who might need to use it. She's not a considerate person. She acts as if her family is a cut above everyone else, but I know that her son—"

"Ethel," her mother interrupted with a gentle smile, "you can never know why people do certain things. If we did understand, perhaps we'd be kinder to them."

Her aunt dropped to her knees to test the Christmas lights, her cheeks flushed at what Louise could tell she thought was a reprimand.

"I just wanted you to know that Daniel might not be able to get through because of a person who doesn't know the meaning of courtesy," she said, sticking the plug into the socket with considerably more force than necessary.

The bulbs didn't light up.

"I didn't mean to sound critical," Mother said. "I guess I'm just a little on edge worrying about Daniel."

"He shouldn't have come," Aunt Ethel said unhappily.

"He came gladly," Mother assured her.

"Oh, I hate these things," Aunt Ethel said. "If one bulb is burnt out, none of them turns on. Are there any spares in the box, Louise?"

Louise found half a dozen loose ones and handed them to her aunt. After seven or eight tries, she found the burnt-out bulb, and the string lit up in a glow of green, yellow, blue and red lights.

Their aunt attached them to the sparse tree limbs using little clips. She worked in silence, accepting Alice's help to hold the string while she continued.

Louise knew her mother hadn't meant to be unkind, but Aunt Ethel's feelings were easily hurt. This wasn't a good Christmas for her either.

"I have to check on the lamb," Aunt Ethel said. "You girls can put the paper stars on the tree."

"Can I come with you?" Alice quickly asked.

Aunt Ethel looked at Mother. She seemed to be biting her tongue.

"You can go," Madeleine said.

When the two had left for the barn, Louise

watched her mother pace through the room and rub her back, at loose ends with nothing to occupy her.

"I should remember how sensitive your aunt is," she confided in Louise.

"Do you think Father is home yet?"

"If your father can't get through on the party line before the service, we might not hear from him until late this evening. I'll feel much better when I know he got home safely."

"Father's a good driver," Louise assured her.

Her mother smiled. "You believe your father can do anything, don't you?" she teased. "But he is a wonderful father and husband."

"And preacher," Louise added. "I'll really miss not hearing his Christmas Eve sermon."

"So will I," Mother wistfully said. "I have an idea. Why don't you play some Christmas songs on your aunt Ethel's piano? I know it's not in tune, but I would like hearing a few of our favorites. There must be some Christmas song sheets in the bench."

"I'll see what I can find," she agreed, although she knew some favorites by heart.

The ivory keys were yellowed with age, and the bench wobbled when Louise sat down. Someone had painted the piano years ago, and the chipped white paint revealed patches of the original varnished finish. As sad as the old piano looked, it sounded worse.

Louise played the first tune that came to her, a spirited rendition of "Jingle Bells." It sounded awful to her, but her mother sat in an easy chair beside the piano and smiled at her efforts.

As hard as Louise tried to concentrate, she couldn't lose herself in music, her usual escape when things bothered her. It was a relief when she heard Aunt Ethel and Alice come back into the kitchen.

"Come see the lamb," Alice cried out. "We brought her inside."

Louise followed her mother to the kitchen and saw the tiny lamb still bundled in the old towel. Alice was holding her with exaggerated care. Aunt Ethel had brought a clothes basket into the kitchen and was busy lining it with more towels.

"The mother won't nurse," Aunt Ethel said with a worried frown. "I thought we could make a temporary bed here. I'll try again to introduce the lamb to the ewe later this evening, but for now, this will save us a lot of trips to the barn. It's getting colder out there, and drifts are piling up."

"I get to feed her," Alice said, waiting impatiently for her aunt to fill the tiny bottle with goat's milk.

She sat down beside the basket where the lamb was softly bleating.

Louise stooped beside her sister, watching with wonder as the tiny creature drank the milk. Alice made little cooing sounds, her happiness making her look even prettier than usual.

The two women sat at the table and watched, both of their faces softened by the poignancy of the scene before them.

"You're doing fine," Aunt Ethel said to Alice. "It takes a gentle touch to care for a newborn lamb."

"Alice is wonderful with animals," Mother said. "I'm blessed to have two daughters who are thoughtful and caring."

"You're very lucky," Aunt Ethel said.

"Yes, I am," their mother agreed. "They're kindhearted and almost always willing to cooperate. I'm going to need their help when their little brother or sister is born."

"I was planning to come when it's your time," Ethel said, still sounding a little hurt. "If you want me, that is."

Mother paused a moment. "Oh, dear, of course I want you." She smiled at Aunt Ethel. "I'm just out of sorts because I'm worried about Daniel."

"You think I'm a bad influence on the girls."

"No, of course not. You are a wonderful, loving aunt, and we're blessed to have you so near. It's just that gossip can be harmful."

"I didn't intend to hurt anyone, but some folks take advantage. Like that woman on our party line."

"I understand. You want to hear that Daniel is safe as much as I do. Maybe you could ask the person to free the line."

"If I interrupt her conversation, she'll leave the phone off the hook just to spite me. I know because she's done it before."

"Then we'll just have to hope she gets tired of talking," Mother said. "I imagine it's frustrating to rely on a party line."

"Yes, it is. I hope someday we'll have a line all to ourselves," Aunt Ethel agreed.

"Meanwhile, we'll just pray Daniel gets home safely even if he can't get through to let us know."

"Look, Mother, the lamb took the whole bottle," Alice said, gently stroking her little head.

"You did a good job," Aunt Ethel complimented her.

"This reminds me of the time when Alice was a newborn," Mother said. "Remember, Ethel, you came to stay with us to help out. You were only a teenager, but you were wonderful with the baby. You even took over the midnight feeding so I could get some rest."

"I was so excited," Aunt Ethel said. "I didn't have much experience with new babies, but your little one made her wants known in no uncertain way. I thought you were the most beautiful thing I'd even seen, Alice. Of course, you were a beauty too, Louise, but I didn't get to take care of you as much as I did your sister."

"I don't know what I would have done without you," Mother said.

"I loved every minute of it," Aunt Ethel assured her. "Daniel always did so much for me. It was my first chance to help him. And you, of course."

"We both appreciated your being there," Mother said with a warm smile on her face. "I believe Daniel was truly worried by the prospect of caring for a toddler and a newborn."

"Oh," Aunt Ethel said suddenly, "I wish I hadn't asked him to come here today. I just panicked, and he's the one person I know I can count on with Bob laid up. Maybe I can repay you if you let me come when the new baby is born."

"Of course," Mother said. "I'll need help more than ever, and Daniel will be so grateful to have you. His congregation keeps him constantly busy."

The two women spontaneously reached across the table and joined hands.

∽

Before Louise realized it, night was upon them, although it wasn't even suppertime.

They played several board games, but Alice paid more attention to the lamb than to Pollyanna or Monopoly. Mother finally begged off, going to the davenport to rest her back. Aunt Ethel, though, had stamina when it came to games. They finally called it a draw when neither one of them could emerge a winner in Monopoly.

Her aunt checked the phone from time to time, and no one was tying up the party line. Louise wished the chatty neighbor was still talking. At least there would be a reason for not hearing from her father. Images of him stuck in a snow bank or lost trying to find a farmhouse to get help popped into her mind.

She prayed silently. It wasn't like her father to keep them in suspense about his whereabouts.

Alice was distracted by the lamb, but her mother and aunt were on edge, stealing glances at the phone as they went about preparing the traditional German Christmas Eve supper.

When Mother was worried, she was very quiet, but Aunt Ethel was just the opposite. She chattered nonstop to cover her nervousness, not seeming to notice that she was the only one talking.

"Uncle Bob's family always makes their own sauerkraut," Aunt Ethel told them. "They put it in big crocks and store it in the cellar to use all winter the way folks did before refrigeration. I bought ours at the grocery store along with the sausages, but I did make *Lebkuchen* on my own."

"What's Lebkuchen?" Alice asked without taking her eyes off the lamb.

"Spicy German cookies. Your uncle loves them. It wouldn't be Christmas for him without them. You boil honey and molasses on the stove, then add brown sugar, egg, lemon juice and lemon zest."

"What's lemon zest?" Louise asked.

"The skin of the lemon finely grated. Just the

yellow part, not the white. You add all that to the dry ingredients, including lots of spice as well as candied citron and chopped hazelnuts. The dough has to chill overnight, then it's rolled out and cut into little rectangles to bake. The last step is frosting the cookies. You're going to love them."

Louise wandered into the parlor and sat down at the piano, but she didn't touch the keys. She wanted to be able to hear the phone if it rang. She had a big lump in her throat when she thought of all the bad things that could have happened to Father out in the storm with that old car.

A shrill ring interrupted her thoughts. Then she heard excited voices and rushed into the kitchen.

"It's Daniel!" Aunt Ethel excitedly told the others. "He couldn't get through before this. The storm must have affected the lines."

"Let me talk," Mother said. "Please."

Aunt Ethel handed her the receiver. "Where are you?" she asked breathlessly.

Her mother's broad smile told Louise all she needed to know. Her father was safe.

When Mother handed her the phone, all Louise could hear was crackling on the line. She reluctantly hung up when it was clear that she wouldn't hear anything else.

"He's been trying to get through all afternoon," Mother said. "The weather made the phone lines erratic, but I'm so thankful he's safe. He had slow going, and he saw several abandoned cars along the way, but our old car got him safely home. The Lord must have been watching over him all the way because the visibility was terrible with swirling snow on the roads."

She turned toward Aunt Ethel, and they hugged each other with relief.

"Thank the Lord," Aunt Ethel said. "First Bob was hurt, then Daniel was missing. I don't know when I've been so nervous."

Alice turned away from the lamb and went to her mother for a hug.

"He'll be here as soon as he can in the morning," Mother said.

Her aunt fixed a tray for Uncle Bob, covering it with a bright red napkin. When she came back from delivering it, she lit creamy beeswax candles on the table and called everyone to take their places.

"Would you like to say a blessing, Madeleine?" she asked.

"It's your home. Why don't you do it?"

Aunt Ethel looked pleased and asked everyone to link hands.

"Blessed Savior, we thank You for the wonder of Your birth, for the plenty we enjoy and for the support of a loving family. Thank You also for protecting Daniel as he traveled to his congregation. We pray in the name of our Lord and Savior Jesus Christ. Amen."

Louise felt a gentle squeeze on her hand and looked up to see her aunt's eyes were moist with emotion.

"That was very nice, Ethel," Mother said.

Louise dug into her supper with gusto, enjoying the spicy meat and fermented cabbage more than she'd expected.

She helped clear the table, not minding that Alice didn't help. Her sister was so enchanted by the lamb that it would have been mean to make her leave its side.

When the dishes were done, Ethel went upstairs to help her husband come down to the parlor where the rest of them waited for him.

"Merry Christmas!" he cried out in his deep bass voice when he saw them. "I'm so glad to see all you lovely ladies."

"Merry Christmas, Uncle Bob," Louise and her sister echoed as he made his way slowly and carefully to the davenport where Ethel had arranged a stack of pillows to support his back. When he was settled, Louise and Alice took turns kissing his cheek and telling him how happy they were to see him downstairs.

Uncle Bob was just the opposite of Aunt Ethel. He had dark hair, warm brown eyes and a strong, square jaw. He was tall and sturdy, dwarfing Aunt Ethel when they stood side by side. Louise thought he was as handsome as a movie star.

"I'm sorry your father can't be with us," he said, "but I'm a lucky man to be surrounded by so many pretty ladies. Tell me, how do you like our lamb, Alice?"

Alice bubbled over with enthusiasm as she described the newborn. She would have brought the lamb into the parlor if Mother, laughing, hadn't discouraged it. "Let the poor little thing sleep. Being born is hard work."

Louise looked at her mother. Was she worried about bringing her own baby into the world?

Uncle Bob was laughing, even though Aunt Ethel was cautioning him not to hurt his back with too much merriment.

"How about you, Louise?" Uncle Bob asked. "Are you ready to play at Carnegie Hall yet?"

She giggled and shook her head.

"In my family, we always read the Christmas story before we open gifts," he said. "Madeleine, would you like to be our reader?"

"I think we'd all like to hear you read it, Bob," her mother said.

"Very well."

Aunt Ethel propped the big family Bible on a pillow in front of him, and he began reading the familiar story.

"Luke chapter two," he began, "'And it came to pass in those days, that there went out a decree from Caesar Augustus that all the world should be taxed....'"

Louise never tired of hearing the story of the Savior's birth.

"'And the angel said unto them,'" Uncle Bob continued, "'"Fear not: for, behold, I bring you good tidings of great joy, which shall be to all people. For unto you is born this day in the city of David a Saviour, which is Christ the Lord. And this shall be a sign unto you; Ye shall find the babe wrapped in swaddling clothes, lying in a manger."'"

When a heavenly host appeared with the angel in the reading, Louise said the words along with her uncle: "'Glory to God in the highest, and on earth peace, good will toward men.'"

When the story concluded with the shepherds visiting the baby Jesus and going forth to spread the good news, everyone in the farmhouse parlor was silent for several moments.

"That was a lovely reading, Bob," Mother finally said.

"Now to light a candle on the tree," Aunt Ethel said, taking a holder from the top of the piano. "Martin Luther decorated his tree with candlelight, and it wouldn't be a German Christmas without candles. But Uncle Bob and I decided last year that one would be enough."

"One carefully watched candle," he said with a smile. "Nothing goes up in flames quicker than a tree that's been sitting inside. Louise, why don't you play a carol while your aunt Ethel helps Alice light it?"

Louise played "O Tannebaum" while Uncle Bob sang a verse in German. He sang a second verse in English, and the others joined in singing "O Christmas Tree."

Louise was so caught up in the mystery of the

Lord's birth and the warmth of the German traditions that she almost forgot they had gifts to open.

Alice passed around everyone's packages, and they took turns opening them. Mother was pleased with a bright red apron with white flowers in the pattern, especially since it had extra long ties that would reach around her up to the time the baby was born. Aunt Ethel had done well by her nieces too. Alice loved her book about farm animals.

"Oh, this is beautiful," Louise said, pinning a sparkly rhinestone brooch on her sweater.

"Just what I need," Uncle Bob said when he opened his package from Alice and Louise to find warm slippers.

Aunt Ethel took special delight in her gift from the family. Mother had knit a long emerald and ivory scarf, just the thing for the frigid winter weather.

"Your uncle and I decided not to exchange our gifts until tomorrow," Ethel explained. "It's going to seem lonely without family after you leave, so we wanted to save something to look forward to."

Uncle Bob led them in a Christmas prayer, then slowly made his way back upstairs, shepherded by his wife.

Alice's eyes were drooping, but she insisted on feeding the lamb again. Louise watched her care for the tiny creature and, at her sister's request, retold the story of Christ's birth.

"I really need to take the lamb back to her mother," Aunt Ethel said, coming into the kitchen a few minutes later. "Goat's milk will keep her from starving, but a lamb needs the immunity from disease that only the ewe can provide."

"I'll go with you!" Alice eagerly offered.

"Perhaps we should all go," Mother said.

"Are you sure you want to go outside?" Louise asked with a worried frown.

"If the Good Lord protected your father all the way to Acorn Hill, I'm sure He'll watch over me on the way to the barn," Mother said with a smile.

They bundled up and put on their boots in the utility room, tramping through the snow behind Aunt Ethel and the little lamb she was holding inside her coat. The storm had subsided, and the wind no longer whipped their faces as they trudged through deep snow. The sky was lit up with countless twinkling stars, and they had no difficulty making their way to the barn.

"I think the sky must have been like this on the

first Christmas Eve," Mother said in a dreamy voice. "I always feel closer to the Lord on a starlit evening like this."

She put her arm around Louise's shoulders as they made their way to the barn door.

The cavernous space didn't seem as cold without the wind battering it. Aunt Ethel put the lamb in the birthing pen and lit the kerosene lantern so they could see better.

Louise held her breath as the tiny creature tottered toward the ewe. The woolly mother didn't seem to react to her offspring, and Alice made a little whimpering noise. They all knew that the lamb was in serious trouble if the ewe rejected it. None of the other ewes had given birth yet, so there was no substitute mother to nurse a rejected lamb.

Alice was so close that the wire of the pen was pressing into her face. She was the first to realize what was happening.

"She's feeding the lamb!" Alice whispered happily.

Alice was right. Mother squeezed Louise's hand as they shared this special moment.

"Well, thank the Lord," Aunt Ethel said with a sigh. "I can't believe what a relief this is."

"Amen," Louise said in a soft voice. Christmas Eve hadn't gone at all the way she'd expected, but she was never going to forget the birth of a lamb on the sacred evening.

They returned to the house with far lighter hearts. Louise was so weary she could have fallen asleep on her feet, but she waited to go upstairs with Alice. She hugged her mother and her aunt and waited patiently while Alice drank a glass of milk and talked nonstop about the lamb.

When her sister finally started up the stairs, Mother whispered to Louise. "Thank you for helping your sister. I never worry when you're with her."

She had wondered how she could do as her father had asked. Now Louise understood that taking responsibility for Alice had been a way to look after her mother too.

As she followed her sister up the stairs, she heard her mother's tinkling laughter and Aunt Ethel's giggle. Christmas Eve at the farm had turned out far better than she'd expected.

True to his word, Father arrived while the family was enjoying an early breakfast of scrambled eggs and cinnamon toast.

"You're a happy group," he said, coming into the kitchen wearing a dark overcoat over his church clothes. His cheeks were red from the cold, and he rubbed his hands together to warm them.

"Father, I got to feed the lamb, but now she's with her mother," Alice said.

"That's wonderful, sweetheart. What about the rest of you? Did you have a nice Christmas Eve?"

"Very nice," Mother said.

"Father, can I have a lamb?" Alice asked.

"I'm afraid a lamb wouldn't be very happy as a house pet," he said, taking her question seriously. "But we'll come back to visit."

"How are the roads?" Mother asked.

"There's drifting in some places, but they're not slippery. We shouldn't have any trouble getting home, but we do have to leave right away if you ladies want to change clothes before the morning service."

"Can I say good-bye to the lamb?" Alice asked in an urgent tone.

"A quick good-bye," her father agreed.

"I'll go with you," Aunt Ethel said. "I need to check on the feed and water."

"I'll run up and wish Bob a blessed Christmas while you get ready to leave," he said to Louise and her mother.

"Well, this isn't a Christmas we'll forget in a hurry," Mother said as she put their gifts into the bag she'd brought with her. "I'm sorry that Christmas Eve was spoiled for you, Louise."

Louise was still sorry she'd missed the caroling and the service at church, but they'd made her aunt and uncle happy by being here, and Alice would never forget holding a newborn lamb. Best of all, they'd shared the love of the Lord together as a family.

"I think this was our best Christmas Eve ever," she assured her mother. "I missed Father, but we got to be with Aunt Ethel and Uncle Bob when they needed us."

"And wasn't it wonderful to have the lamb born on the eve of our Savior's birth," Mother said with a contented smile.

She hugged her daughter, then urged her to put on her coat so they could leave.

She and her mother laughed together just because it felt so good to have Father with them.

"Did I miss something funny?" Father asked as he came into the kitchen.

"A little lamb shall lead them," Mother said with a broad smile. "It brought us to the farm, and that was a good thing."

"This is truly a happy Christmas," Louise decided.

$\mathcal{I}$t *was* a happy Christmas, wasn't it?" Alice said.

"I remember my first sight of that lamb. What a miracle. And her arrival on Christmas Eve, the tiny newborn made the birth of Jesus seem more real to me. I don't recall all those other details, though."

Louise smiled. "You were so busy taking care of that lamb, it's a wonder you remember anything else."

"I loved Heiligabend."

"I remember Heiligabend," Jane said. "I played with her when we visited the farm. Weirdest name for a lamb I ever heard."

"It means 'Christmas Eve' in German," Alice said. "I was oblivious to your concern about Mother and Father, Louise. You must have been exasperated with me."

"A bit, but I understood. And really, it was better that you weren't worried too." Louise smiled. "That lamb became everyone's pet. Remember how Jane would run to see her when we'd visit the farm?"

"I do. We have a picture of you riding her, Jane." Rising, Alice retrieved an album from the built-in cupboard. "In this one, I think."

Alice sat on the couch next to Jane and opened the album. Louise came over to see.

"There's Aunt Ethel by the barn. Wow. Look at her hairdo. And those crazy black-and-white striped bell-bottoms. Sure doesn't look like farm wear," Jane said.

"She liked to be fashionable. Bouffant hairstyles were all the rage. She backcombed it and poked it with a pick to get it to pouf out, then she'd spray it," Louise said. "I could never make mine look right."

Another photo showed Louise at twenty, in a calf-length gray skirt with her dark hair pulled up in a French twist and her baby-blue cardigan sweater pushed up on her forearms.

"That's you, isn't it, Alice?" Jane pointed to the teenager with a simple bob haircut in a forest-green A-line dress.

"Yes, that's me. I remember loving that dress. I wore it until the lining started to give way." Alice turned the page, then pointed to a little girl in dark pigtails. "There you are."

Sure enough, Jane was straddling a large ewe while Ethel held it by a rope.

"You had to be about six. Look at your toothless grin."

Jane giggled. "I looked like Pollyanna, didn't I?"

"*Pollyanna* was your favorite movie," Louise said, smiling.

"Oh yeah. I remember." Jane turned several pages in the album, laughing at their clothes and hairdos.

When Alice put the album away and they resumed their seats, Jane sighed. "That was your last Christmas with Mother. No wonder it's a special Christmas memory. I wish I had just one memory of being with her."

Louise reached over and patted Jane's hand. "I wish so too, but she lives on in us. I see her gentle sweetness in both of you. Alice has her gift of mercy, caring for people in need, and you have her gift of hospitality, making people comfortable and serving them in our home. But, in addition to being special because it was Mother's last Christmas with us, I learned something important that Christmas Eve on the farm."

"That Alice was meant to take care of helpless creatures?" Jane asked, teasing.

"That Christmas lives in our hearts, not in a place. I wanted desperately to get home, but I'd never felt the love of our Lord more than when the storm kept us at the farm. Father wasn't with us that night, but I felt his presence, as I do now that he's passed on."

"God answered your prayers and kept Father safe," Jane said.

"He kept the lamb safe too," Alice added. "The lamb's surviving was my best present that year. I was praying the lamb would be all right without Father being there to take care of her. Aunt Ethel didn't have much experience, and Uncle Bob was hurt, so he couldn't help."

"The farm was a great place to learn to rely on the Lord," Louise said.

"Difficulties tend to increase our faith," Alice said. "I remember a Christmas that really challenged me, but it turned out to be an amazing blessing, one that continues to inspire me today."

"Really? What was that?" Jane asked. "Tell us, please?" Jane leaned against the armrest and looked at Alice expectantly.

Alice's Christmas Memory

Bing Crosby or the Carpenters? On the fourth day of December, Alice deliberated between two cassette tapes.

In the end the oldies called to her. Even though it was 1980, she still enjoyed the nostalgic sound of Bing Crosby's Christmas songs. As she sat at the kitchen table to write her Christmas cards, she sang along with *Bing Crosby's Christmas Classics.* Her cards were illustrated with a painting of a white clapboard church in a deep winter snow. She had been drawn to the cards because the image was reminiscent of Grace Chapel, the little church where her father was the pastor.

The telephone rang as she finished the *As* in her address book. "I'll get it, Father."

"Thank you." The answer drifted back to her from the study, where Father was working on Sunday's sermon.

Alice tossed back her wedge-cut soft red hair as she lifted the receiver. "Hello?" With the extra-long cord on the handset, she was able to walk back to the table and get out the next card while she spoke.

"Hello, Alice. This is Cathy Carling."

"Hi, Cathy." The young woman was the director of the children's musical that would be a part of the Christmas Eve service. "How are you?"

"Not so great." Cathy's voice quavered.

"What's wrong?" Alice asked gently.

"My mother had a stroke this morning," Cathy told her. "She lives in Minnesota, and I must get there right away."

Alice was instantly sympathetic. "I'm so sorry to hear that. Would you like to speak to my father?"

"No, but would you ask him to pray for her?"

"We both will," Alice assured her.

"Actually, you're the one I want to speak to, Alice."

"How can I help?"

Cathy hesitated. "I need someone to run tomorrow's meeting for the Christmas musical. It's the first meeting and—"

"Oh, Cathy, I don't have a theatrical bone in my body." The request was far out of Alice's comfort zone.

"You wouldn't really be directing anything, and it's just for one night. Please, Alice? It would ease my mind so much."

Alice felt herself frowning and consciously smoothed out her expression. "Surely there's someone better suited. I don't have much experience with groups of children, and I have even less with music and drama."

"I've already tried half a dozen people. The choir director's got laryngitis. Everyone else who sings or acts is busy."

Perhaps, Alice thought, she should feel insulted that she was clearly at the bottom of the list. But if she were Cathy, only sheer desperation would drive her to call someone like herself.

"Please, Alice," Cathy implored. "The kids usually have plenty of ideas —"

"Ideas for what, exactly?"

"The musical. They create the script and choose the music. I have a couple of idea books and a cassette of appropriate Christmas music. They'll need to select a few songs to sing."

Alice knew there was no way she could manage a meeting like that. She would simply say no. But Alice couldn't turn away from somebody in need.

"All right," she heard herself say meekly.

"Wonderful!" Relief rolled over the connection. "Thanks so much, Alice. I'll drop off the materials before I leave town."

The following evening, Alice walked to the nearby chapel to lead the first meeting for the Christmas musical. As she unlocked the door and laid out the materials, her throat felt tight with apprehension.

This is silly, she told herself. *You know all of these children from church.* But she had never tried to teach any sizable group.

As the children began to arrive, Alice's hands were shaking. She gripped them tightly before her, greeting each child. As she did so, she repeatedly asked the parents dropping them off if they could stay to help. But everyone, it seemed, had other activities.

"Alice!"

She turned at the sound of her name to see Tina Carsten steaming toward her, towing her daughter Kimmy in her wake. Tina was a solidly built woman with a strong personality. On a number of occasions, Alice knew her father had been forced to mediate disagreements for various committees on which Tina had served. She had good ideas, but her need to take charge had alienated more than one parishioner.

In contrast, Tina's youngest daughter was sweet, exceptionally agreeable and quiet.

"Hello, Tina. Hello, Kimmy. I'm glad you're joining us."

"Where's Cathy?" Tina dispensed with a greeting and looked around, brows drawn together.

"Cathy was called out of town," Alice said. She smiled, hoping she projected confidence.

"Do you know anything about acting?" Tina asked.

Alice shook her head. "Cathy's options were limited. But I'm just here for the first meeting. She'll be back soon. Besides, the children will be putting together the program. I promise you I'll do my best to help them."

Tina tossed her head impatiently. "Okay, then I need to talk to you about Kimmy's solos."

"All right." Alice glanced at the notes she had made as she reviewed Cathy's materials. "I didn't recall that there were solos."

"There are solos every year. Kimmy should have one, and the lead," her mother said, propelling Kimmy forward with a hand between the girl's shoulder blades. "She's far too shy. Her older sisters used to be the same way."

"I'm not *shy*, Mom." Kimmy rolled eyes. "I just don't feel like I need the lead in every play we do."

"You need opportunities to develop stage presence," Tina said briskly. "There's nothing worse than being afraid to get up in front of a crowd."

Alice glanced at the girl. She didn't look at all excited about the chance to "develop stage presence."

"I'll see what I can do," she told Tina. "The final call will be up to the children."

Tina frowned. "Children can't make decisions like that."

Alice glanced at her watch. "Gracious! We need to get started. You'll have to excuse me, Tina." Sometimes, she decided as she beat a retreat across the room, there was just nothing one could say to defuse a situation. Escape was the only option.

Alice clapped her hands and ushered the milling group of children to their seats.

"All right!" she said brightly, when each child had found a chair. "Miss Carling had to go out of town...," and she went on to explain Cathy's absence. "So I'm going to be helping you with your script and music choices tonight." There were no protests, and her nerves began to settle as she popped the cassette Cathy had given her into the portable player.

As the first notes of music began to fill the room, she saw Mark Trimble and Robert Pfiffer jabbing each other in the ribs with pencils. Without speaking, she walked back and confiscated the pencils. The boys settled down immediately, and she congratulated herself on solving a potential problem. The Trimble boy was the youngest of several brothers, all of whom were known for their inability to sit still.

As the music wore on, other children became restless. Finally, Alice stopped the tape player. "Let's take a break." She suppressed a sigh as the roomful of children exploded into motion.

The children reconvened a few minutes later. "Now," Alice said, "you've heard a number of songs. We need to choose a few that you would like to sing, and then we'll write our script, our story, around those. Who had a favorite?"

Seventeen sets of eyes stared at her. No one spoke. No one even raised a hand. "Oh, come on," she said. "I know there must have been some that you liked better than others."

Still nothing. "All right. If none of you has a favorite, I'll choose." Deliberately, she suggested a draggy piece that she suspected the children wouldn't pick. "How about 'He's Coming'?"

"Yuck. I don't like that one," Ellen Sizemore said.

"I'm open to a better suggestion," Alice told her.

Ellen grimaced. "I guess 'Let There Be Peace on Earth' isn't too bad."

"How do the rest of you feel about that choice?" Alice asked, looking around and getting no reaction.

"Great!" Even she could hear the false cheer in her voice. "Any more suggestions?"

Silence again.

"I want to do 'Hark the Herald Angels Sing,'" Pauline Meek suddenly said.

"We sang that last year *and* the year before," Julia Anderstrand grumbled.

"Well," Alice said. "Which songs haven't you done?"

It was like pulling teeth, but finally they had a list of songs. Now for the skit. Alice clapped her hands and the chattering children grew quiet. "You did a wonderful job with that," she said. "I think you deserve a game break."

"A game break?" several voices inquired.

"How about Bible charades? You can act out characters from Bible stories."

Quickly, she divided the children into three teams and handed Celeste paper and pen. "Celeste and Kimmy, you're the oldest, so you explain the rules and get the game started. I'm going to talk with a few people."

"Here." Celeste thrust the writing implements at Kimmy. "I'll divide up teams if you choose the characters."

Alice stood near the back of the room where she could supervise, noting that Celeste and Kimmy were proving surprisingly adept at managing the younger children. Then she asked Pauline Meek to join her.

"I need ideas," Alice whispered dramatically, as Pauline approached. "My idea well has gone dry." She would accomplish two tasks at once, Alice decided, getting script ideas and also seeing which children might be best suited for speaking roles in the play.

But when Pauline rejoined the group a few

minutes later, she hadn't given Alice much inspiration for a topic. Perhaps the others would have some thoughts. After Alice had interviewed several children, Celeste Rockwell was next. Tall for a twelve-year-old, Celeste was outgoing and friendly.

Alice handed her the paper with the lines she had the older children reading to "audition." "Here you go. Read over these, and then act them out for me."

Celeste grimaced. "Why don't you just tell me what you want me to say? It'll help if I hear the lines out loud first."

Shrugging inwardly, Alice complied.

When Celeste spoke the lines, she did so with an assurance that made Alice realize the girl was a natural onstage. But she wasn't a great help with script ideas, nor were any of the other children who followed her. Fearing she was going to be forced to write something herself, Alice called the last child's name.

"Hi, Kimmy. Any ideas for this script?"

"I thought you'd never ask." Kimmy Carsten's delivery was deadpan, and Alice laughed.

"You were doing such a great job with the younger ones that I hated to interrupt you." Alice paused. "So you have an idea?"

Kimmy met her eyes. "I'll only share it if you promise I don't have to play the lead."

"You don't want the lead?"

Kimmy shook her head. "Celeste would love it, though."

At this point, Alice figured there was nothing to lose. Tina might not be happy, but Kimmy would. And Celeste would be good in a primary role. "It's a deal."

"Okay." Kimmy opened a folder and laid it on the table, squaring the papers within it neatly. "What if we did 'The Gift of the Magi,' but made it in the present day? I had to write a story in English class based on something we studied during the year, and that's the one I chose. I thought we could make it into a script, so I brought it tonight."

Alice sucked in her breath. "That's a *great* idea! A contemporary version sounds like fun. Where would you set it?"

"In a neighborhood. That way, there would be parts for all the kids."

"In the original story by O. Henry, a young married couple has very little money. Each of them sells a prized possession in order to buy a gift for the other," Alice said. "But when they exchange gifts, they find that they have bought each other items that they can no longer use, items that were to be used with the things they sold. How did you do that in your story?"

Kimmy suddenly looked intensely animated. "I had two sisters who wanted to get gifts for each other. Each of them had to give up something they really treasured to buy the other sister's gift."

Clearly, Alice thought, *creativity and imagination are this girl's lifeblood*. Aloud, she said, "That sounds great, but why would they do it? Sisters sometimes fight, you know."

Kimmy grinned. She was the youngest of three girls. "I know. Do you have sisters?"

Alice nodded, a pang of regret filling her. She saw little of Jane, who lived in California. Louise was much closer, but even they didn't visit much. Alice and her father were usually tied up with church concerns on weekends, while Louise, her husband Eliot and daughter Cynthia lived busy lives in Philadelphia. Happily, they all were coming home the weekend before Christmas and planned to stay through the holiday to the following Thursday. "I have two sisters, just like you," she answered. "Except that I'm the middle sister instead of the youngest." She smiled. "I love them very much."

"That's why they would do it." Kimmy sounded

certain. "The sisters in the story, I mean. The reason they would give up something very special for the other is because they love each other so much."

A ruckus from one of the charades teams caught Alice's attention. "Excuse me a minute." Walking over to the team, she saw that the two boys who had been silly earlier were at it again. Walking over to the group, she said, "How's it going here?"

Several children began to speak at once, and she cautioned them with a raised hand. "One at a time, please."

As the children subsided and began to take turns talking, Alice maneuvered her way over to where Mark Trimble and Robert Pfiffer were pushing each other. She placed a hand on each boy's shoulder as she listened to their teammates. Like magic, the wriggling children stood still.

"Thank you, boys," she said to them when there was a break in the conversation. "It's hard to think when there's a lot of noise in the room." She glanced at the other team. "You'd better get hopping. Looks like they're two points ahead of you!"

"Let's go!" Mark said. He turned his attention to the game with an intensity that made Alice smile as she moved away. If Mark and Robert gave the charades the energy they did their misbehavior, the other team didn't stand a chance.

"I think I could write our script, Miss Howard," Kimmy said, coming to her side, "if you help me."

"Oh, Kimmy, that would be fantastic." Alice's response was heartfelt. "Tell you what: you write a first draft, and then you and I can get together and polish it a little before you show it to Miss Carling."

"How about Saturday afternoon?" Kimmy asked. "Tomorrow's Friday, and I'm leaving school early to go to the dentist, so I'll have extra time. If I start it tonight, it should be done by Saturday."

"And you know how to write a play?"

Kimmy nodded. "I wrote one for my class last spring and one for my English teacher this fall." She squared her shoulders proudly. "I got As on both of them."

Thank You, dear Lord. Alice's prayer was fervent. *You saw my need, and You provided.*

∽

"Alice!" The critical care supervisor beckoned to her the moment she arrived on the floor Friday morning. Millie, the supervisor, held up a chart and waggled it. "We just admitted a critical patient who came into the ER and was taken to ortho surgery. Her car was hit by a truck running a red light." Millie handed Alice the chart. "Her toddler wasn't hurt, thank goodness, but the mother has broken bones in both arms. One's a simple, but she shattered the other in several places."

Alice looked over the chart in dismay. "And she has a little one? Oh, poor thing. It's going to be awhile before she can do much for the child again." She began to walk toward the patient's room "I'll just stick my head in and say hello if she's awake."

The patient, Suzanne McCann, appeared to be awake, blinking groggily, when Alice entered her room.

"Hello there, Suzanne. I'm Alice." She took the left wrist, checking her pulse. "I'm going to be your nurse today. If you need anything, you just press this." Alice indicated the call button.

"I'm Suzy...Alice." Tears began to roll down her cheeks. "Where's Beth?"

Alice gently took Suzy's hand. "Is Beth your daughter?"

"Yes...I...where's Beth?"

"Beth is fine," Alice assured her, recalling Millie's words. "Would you like me to find out where she is?"

"Please call my mother," Suzy said. "I'm pretty sure someone in the ER told me that Mom has Beth."

"All right." Alice quietly hung the chart at the foot of the bed. She had just started down the hall when a well-padded woman with gray in her dark hair walked toward the nurses' desk. She carried a little dark-haired girl, and as she reached Alice, she said anxiously, "I'm Liz Henshaw. My daughter's here— Suzanne McCann? Do you know where she is?"

Alice smiled and led the woman toward Suzy's room. "I just spoke with her, Ms. Henshaw. She's worried about Beth."

"Mommy huwt," the little girl told Alice.

Alice nodded. "I know. But we're going to make her better."

⌒

Alice and her father lingered over dinner that evening. He had been on a pastoral call the night before when she'd arrived home from the pageant meeting, and she'd left early this morning before he'd been awake.

Father took the last bite of his tuna-noodle casserole and sat back in his chair. His once-dark hair gleamed a shining silver in the glow of the overhead light. "Wonderful meal, as always." He smiled at her.

As she removed his dinner plate, Alice leaned down and kissed his cheek. "Thank you, Father."

"How did your rehearsal go yesterday evening?" Father asked, as she poured his coffee. "I meant to ask before, but I'm afraid I hijacked the conversation, didn't I?" They had spent most of the meal discussing ways to help the family of the ill parishioner with whom he had visited last night.

Alice laughed and recapped the experience for him, embellishing the antics of the lively younger boys.

The ringing of the telephone interrupted them. Alice rose and answered the phone.

"Alice, hi. It's Cathy."

"Hi, Cathy. How's your mother doing?"

"Not very well. Alice, I have to take Mom to rehab, oversee some renovations to make her house easier for her to get around and find some part-time help to care for her at home. It looks like I'll be here for several weeks." Before Alice could speak, Cathy rushed on. "I know it's a huge imposition, but could you possibly continue to lead the musical production?"

Alice wanted to say no, but of course she couldn't. Cathy's mother was ill, and Alice knew the last thing Cathy needed was to worry about a church play halfway across the country. "Of course," she said. "I'll do what I can, but you know my limitations."

"I bet you'll surprise yourself," Cathy said. "Thank you so much, Alice. You can't imagine how much this relieves my mind."

"Don't worry about anything. You just concentrate on spending time with your mother. My father and I will continue to pray for you both."

After she hung up the telephone, she told her father, "Cathy Carling's not coming back until after Christmas." Her voice shook as she added, "I told her I'd take care of the play. Oh, Father, I'm not sure I'm up to it."

"I bet if you visit the library, you can find a book or two that might offer some insights. And Alice, you're not alone. 'Trust in the Lord with all your heart and lean not on your own understanding; in all your ways acknowledge Him, and He will make your paths straight.'"

She tried to smile, recognizing the quote from Proverbs 3. "I'll do what I can, Father."

Her father smiled. "I have every confidence in you. With the Lord's help, you can manage this."

Still, Alice continued to feel troubled and anxious while she cleaned up the dishes and did a few more chores. Later, after donning her pajamas and preparing for bed, she recalled her father's advice. "Dear Lord," she said before she concluded her prayers, "fill me with patience to manage the children during rehearsals. And please guide me to find some resources that will enhance my abilities. You know my limits even better than I."

She climbed into bed. As she closed her eyes, she realized that the anxious beat of her heart had calmed, and peace filled her.

On Saturday, Alice took the time for a walk with one of her closest friends, Vera Humbert.

"I heard about Cathy's mother," Vera said. "And that you're taking over the Christmas show."

Alice shrugged. "There just wasn't anyone else. I hope my efforts won't be judged against some of the stellar productions from the past."

Vera smiled. "I'm sure everyone will be grateful that you stepped in so willingly. And if anyone is critical, that's a reflection on him or her rather than you."

"Tina Carsten isn't going to be happy with me. She wanted Kimmy to have a lead role, but Kimmy didn't want one, and I'm not going to force her."

"*Phf-f-f-t.*" Vera made a dismissive sound. "Ignore Tina. The way she carries on, you'd never know she was as shy as a church mouse when she was young."

"The Tina Carsten I know?" Alice was incredulous.

Vera chuckled. "One and the same. I think that's why she's so determined to push her girls into the spotlight."

"That explains a lot." Alice was thoughtful. "But Kimmy's not shy, she just knows what she wants, and what she wants isn't performing."

"Stick to your guns," Vera said. "I had two of her girls in my classroom, and she frequently felt the need to explain my job to me."

Alice chuckled. "If she can explain how to settle down a group of rowdy kids, I might listen."

She shared her experiences with the Trimble and Pfiffer boys.

"Alice, it sounds to me as if you did exactly the right things." Vera's tone was reassuring. "A teacher's proximity to a student can change behavior very effectively without that teacher ever having to say a word. And I think giving them a chance to 'shake their sillies out' with games is a great idea. There are different opinions on how long children's attention spans are—generally the younger the child, the shorter the lesson needs to be—but I can guarantee you that no child is happy about sitting in a chair for more than an hour. Your instincts are excellent." Vera smiled. "You should be teaching."

Alice shook her head with vigor. "No thank you. I do enjoy some aspects of working with children, and I wish I had more opportunities. Just not," she added emphatically, "by directing a musical!"

Kimmy Carsten arrived shortly after lunch Saturday afternoon. The girl settled at the kitchen table while Alice made hot chocolate and then took a seat. "So how did your writing go?"

Kimmy's thin face lit up. "Great! At least, it seems

pretty good to me." She passed the folder to Alice, who bent her head to the script, silently praying there were some useable parts. Kimmy was going to be crushed if there weren't.

Ten minutes later, Alice lifted her head. "Kimmy!" Alice didn't even try to hide the real joy in her tone. "This is excellent. Incredible. Does your mother know you write like this?"

Kimmy ducked her head. "Yes." There was an unspoken "but," and Alice assumed that in Tina Carsten's world, great writing skills were not as highly valued as performance arts.

Alice tapped the script. There would need to be a few changes, but Alice could handle those. "It really is terrific." She grinned. "And I see you've written it to include something for everyone."

Kimmy nodded. "That's what most school plays do."

"And you have spread the solos around."

Kimmy nodded. "That's the way it should be." She hesitated. "I guess I'd better take one so my mom doesn't have a fit."

Alice nodded. "A wise decision."

The following Friday, a week after Suzy McCann's accident, Alice visited her room. "Good morning. Are you being discharged today?"

"I think so." Suzy looked worried rather than relieved. "I'm anxious to get home. Beth is sick."

"Oh dear. What's wrong?"

"I don't know. Mom said she's running a fever and has a stuffy nose."

Alice frowned. "Perhaps she shouldn't bring Beth to the hospital today."

"She's not."

"If your mother's not picking you up, how are you getting home?"

"Taxi— Holy cow!" Suzy's exclamation was more of a groan. "I just realized I can't even dial the phone. Could you call me a cab if I'm discharged?"

Alice smiled. "Why don't we skip the taxi. If you get the green light for discharge, I can take you home when I get off my shift. "

Suzy looked stunned. "Are you certain you want to do that? I don't want to be an imposition."

"You aren't," Alice assured her. "I'm happy to do it."

Later that afternoon Suzy was discharged, and Alice brought her car around to the front of the hospital. When they arrived at the McCann home, Liz looked harassed. "Hello, Alice. Thank you so much for bringing Suzy home."

Alice smiled. "My pleasure." As a fussy cry rang out from farther inside the house, she glanced over Liz's shoulder in concern. "I understand Beth is sick. Is it something Suzy could catch?"

"Oh no." She addressed her next words to her daughter. "Honey, Beth has chicken pox."

Suzy's whole body sagged. "That's terrible. I can't even hold her." She peered anxiously at Alice. "You have had the chicken pox, haven't you? Mom and I both have."

"I had them when I was little," Alice said. "Is there anything I can do?"

"Not unless you have a better remedy than calamine lotion," Liz said.

"Oatmeal baths are helpful," Alice said. "And keeping her cool. The warmer she is, the worse the itching. Scratching will produce scarring, so you want to prevent that as much as possible."

"Yes," Liz said, "I put mittens on her little hands today to keep her from digging at the pox."

Alice nodded. "That's a good idea."

Another cry sounded from inside the house, and Liz turned and dashed away.

Alice helped Suzy take off her coat and find a seat in the living room. The bulky casts on both arms made the process difficult. Suzy was going to get plenty of practice with patience in the next few weeks, Alice predicted with sympathy.

When she had finished retrieving Suzy's belongings from her car, Alice entered the living room to find Suzy crying. The young mother lifted her free arm—the other was secured in a sling across her torso—and tried to wipe away tears, despite the cast that covered the area up to above her elbow. "I've never been so frustrated in my entire life." Her breath hitched. "I just want to make it better, and I can barely even touch her."

"Let me dash to the store," Alice said. "Oatmeal baths really do help, and if I go now, Beth could be getting some relief from that itching fairly soon."

Suzy's eyes widened. "Really? Oh, thank you, Alice."

Less than fifteen minutes later, Alice handed a box of oatmeal baths to Suzy's mother, who took it and hurried away.

"How badly is she affected?" Alice asked Suzy when they were alone.

"They're mostly on her back and her chest. A few on her arms and legs. None on her face so far. Poor Mom, having to deal with that *and* an invalid."

Alice nodded sympathetically. "She is going to have her hands full." She glanced around, noting a small undecorated tree in one corner. She could imagine how overwhelmed Liz must feel, trying to care for both her daughter and granddaughter. "Maybe I could work on the tree for a bit before I go," she suggested.

When Suzy approved the idea, Alice pulled out a box shoved into the corner. "Why don't you tell me where you want things, and I'll be your arms."

Suzy smiled, and the lines of tension on her forehead eased. "Thanks, Alice."

Half an hour later, Beth toddled into the living room with Liz behind her. "See?" She pointed at Suzy. "Mommy's home."

The tiny girl made a beeline for her mother, gleefully climbing into her lap, heedless of the casts. Alarmed, Liz rushed over and attempted to pluck her away.

"It's okay, Mom," Suzy said, although Alice noticed her grimace with pain.

Alice reached into the shopping bag she'd gotten when she went to get the oatmeal baths and pulled out a book. "Beth?" she said. "I have a present for you. Do you like stories?"

"'Tory!" she said. She twisted and patted her mother's cheek. "Read 'tory?"

"I'll listen, and Grammy can read."

Liz sank into a second chair she had positioned beside Suzy's. "And Mommy can listen with you."

The story was a child's version of the Christmas story, beautifully illustrated in watercolors. Alice was delighted by the little girl's total absorption in the tale. When Liz finished the book, Alice said, "I have something else."

Alice held up the item she'd been working on during the story. "It's an Advent calendar," she said. "Advent's already begun, but that's okay. I thought it might be a nice way to keep the meaning of the season front and center."

"That's a lovely thought, Alice." Liz took the calendar from Alice and held it where Beth could reach it, and the three of them explored the first several days. Each day had a door with a small box behind it for little gifts. Alice had filled the first few with treats, leaving the others for Suzy and Liz to fill.

"This is so thoughtful of you," Suzy said. "Thank you so much, Alice. You must have children of your own."

"No." Alice laughed, recalling her most recent interactions with children. "But right now I'm standing in as a director for our church children's musical, and I've had a crash course in managing elementary schoolers."

"Oh boy," Liz said. "That can be interesting. I used to be a teacher's aide in a fifth-grade classroom. At that age, they're either angels or devils."

"Honestly, all of the children in the play are good kids. A couple of the boys get silly when they spend time together, but now I separate them. My biggest problem," she went on, "is that I don't know enough about music or theater. The show is less than two weeks away, and we are nowhere near close to being ready." She forced back the panic that threatened every time she thought of the musical. Despite the stellar script, rehearsal had gone poorly on Sunday. It seemed to take forever to accomplish a tiny bit.

"What's the play about?" Liz asked.

Alice explained Kimmy's idea and told them what a gifted writer the child was. "She has saved my sanity," Alice said. "Who knows what might have happened if I had been compelled to write that script myself!"

$\backsim$

"Hello?" Alice answered the telephone in the kitchen. Ever since Cathy's second call, she had approached the phone with trepidation, certain it was going to be something else to add to her crazy schedule.

"Hello, dear." The voice was rich and melodious and wonderfully familiar.

"Louise! Hello. How are you? How are Eliot and Cynthia?"

"Everyone's fine," her elder sister reported. "I talked with Father earlier today, but I wanted to speak with you."

Alice sank down at the table, twirling the long phone cord around her fingers. "It's so good to hear your voice. I'm sorry I haven't called since we came to Cynthia's show. It's been hectic here." She thought of the upcoming holiday. "Are you still planning to arrive on the twentieth?"

"That's right, a week from today."

"Oh dear." Alice couldn't hide her dismay as a thought occurred.

"I beg your pardon?" Louise sounded taken aback.

"That means you'll be here for the church musical on Sunday the twenty-first."

There was a momentary pause on Louise's end. "You don't want us to see the play this year?"

The question was all it took for Alice to unburden herself to her sister. A music educator in the Philadelphia area, Louise was a gifted pianist and organist, and her husband was a respected professor of music. If anyone understood directing a performance, it was Louise.

"Oh, Alice," Louise said when she had finished. "It sounds as if you're handling it well, given the circumstances. Some people would just curl up in a little ball if you threw them into a roomful of children."

That elicited a chuckle. "I like the children. It's the music and stage stuff that's got me in a dither."

$\backsim$

An hour after Sunday evening's rehearsal began, Alice felt ready to quit, except that doing so would disappoint her father.

Celeste, who had taken on the bulk of the lines and one solo, insisted that she'd been working on memorizing her part, but it surely didn't show. The poor child couldn't remember any of her lines, and the solo was as appallingly off-key as before.

Alice assumed her most encouraging expression. "You'll get it," she said.

But Celeste grew increasingly frustrated as the rehearsal ground on, and by the time her mother arrived, the girl was nearly in tears.

Alice felt terrible. "Do you think it's too stressful for her?" she asked Celeste's mother.

"Oh no," Mrs. Rockwell said cheerfully. "Because of her learning disabilities, Celeste rarely gets any substantial parts in school or church performances. She's thrilled with the opportunity. We'll just keep plugging away at the lines, and eventually she'll get them, just like she does spelling words and math equations. The singing, well, I can't make any promises other than that she'll know the words." She winked. "Poor kid takes after me. I'm tone deaf."

As the words sank in, Alice forced her lips to turn up in a sickly smile. Learning disabilities! It might have been nice if someone had shared that bit of information with her.

Mrs. Rockwell reached out to clasp Alice's hand. "Thank you, Miss Howard, for giving her a chance."

"You're welcome." Finally, Alice knew what to say. "We'll both keep working with her. She's going to do just fine."

Her father met her at the door Tuesday evening after another rehearsal with a steaming cup of her favorite tea and a gentle smile. "I thought you might like something warm to drink."

"Oh, thank you," she exclaimed, shucking off her coat and hanging it on a hook by the kitchen door. "This is exactly what I need." She followed her father to his office and sank down into a comfortable armchair.

"How did it go today?" Father asked.

Alice made a helpless gesture with her free hand, giving him the highlights. "And Tina Carsten is going to be furious with me because I assigned the lead to Celeste."

Father made a noncommittal sound. "It's a

wonderful opportunity for Celeste. And if Kimmy truly doesn't want to be in the spotlight, no amount of pushing from her mother is going to do any good."

"I hope Tina will be able to see what a gifted writer Kimmy is. How many sixth graders could have written that script?"

Father nodded. "It sounds as if Kimmy has quite a flair for storytelling. So how did the rest of the rehearsal go?"

"Terrible." Alice groaned. "Father, I'm not at all sure I can pull this together. The boys continue to be silly and distracting unless I am watching them every second."

"If it gets really bad, you might consider asking their parents to sit in on a rehearsal."

"I may try that," she said. "But I'm not sure what to do about the other problem. Celeste Rockwell, bless her heart, can't carry a tune."

"That is a problem." Father chuckled, shaking his head. "Still, the congregation won't care. Much."

"I care," Alice said. "And so does Celeste. She got very upset with herself this afternoon. She can't match my pitch, can't sing a melody in *any* key, and she can't read music—or words, for that matter—

so she's often lost when it's her turn to sing. I don't have a clue how to help her."

Father cleared his throat. "That sounds like a challenge even Louise might struggle with."

"Are you *sure* we can't cancel this? Or at least postpone it until Cathy's return?"

Father shook his head, and the light glanced off his horn-rimmed spectacles. "I would really hate to do that. The congregation loves our children's Christmas musical tradition. But I may have something that will help a little...or perhaps I should say some*one*." Clearing his throat, her father turned and glanced at the door of the study.

Alice shifted in her seat, following his gaze.

There stood...*Louise*! Alice scrambled out of her seat, barely managing to set down her tea, before she ran across the room and threw her arms around her sister. "Oh, it's good to see you! What are you *doing* here?"

Louise laughed, the sound muffled by Alice's stranglehold. "I thought you could use help with your musical," she said after Alice set her loose. "My big holiday commitment was last night, so I decided to come home a few days early."

Alice's mouth fell open. "Really? You're here for good?" As her sister nodded, tears welled up. "This might be one of the most wonderful surprises I've ever had! Merry Christmas to *me*!"

Wednesday, Alice had the day off. She practically bounced down the stairs to start breakfast.

"Good morning." Louise wandered in a few moments later.

"Good morning."

Louise went straight to the refrigerator to peruse the offerings, finally extracting the orange juice. "So what's on your agenda today?"

"I'm free." Alice threw her arms wide. "If you're serious about helping with this musical, we can use the entire day."

"It's a deal."

As they ate breakfast, they caught up on each other's lives. Afterward, they dressed and walked over to the church.

Inside the Assembly Room, Louise looked around with a frown. "There used to be a piano in here."

"Yes." Alice chuckled. "When we were children.

It's been gone for years. We don't need one, though. All the music is recorded, and I have a portable cassette player."

Louise laughed. "I think not. I will never use a recording for a live performance."

"But that's all I have available," Alice protested.

"Are they doing familiar songs?"

"Well, yes, but—"

"What are they?"

Alice pulled a piece of paper from the folder in which she carried her script. "Here We Come A-Caroling," "All Through the Night" and "Let There Be Peace on Earth."

Louise's eyebrows rose, and she nodded approvingly. "Lovely choices. Unusual for a Christmas play, but I suppose they do all express a Christian sentiment, don't they?"

Alice smiled. "They do. In the story—"

"You can tell me later. Right now, I'm most concerned about the music. I wish I'd known there was no piano down here. I would have brought my electric keyboard."

"There's a piano in the sanctuary now," Alice said. "In fact, it might be the same old one you remember."

Louise shuddered. "I hope not."

"It's never used anymore."

"Well, it's about to be." Louise walked toward the door. "Let's go upstairs, and I'll start working out arrangements."

Alice followed Louise into the sanctuary and to the front where the old piano stood along a side wall. Drawing off the dust cover, Louise pulled out the bench and sat.

She lifted the lid and arched her fingers, then firmly played the first chord.

Louise yanked her fingers up off the keys. Even Alice, who claimed no musical expertise, could hear the dissonance.

"I guess it's a little out of tune," Alice said.

"A little?" Louise looked utterly horrified. She pinched the bridge of her nose between thumb and forefinger. "All right," she said. "Eliot and Cynthia weren't coming until Saturday. But if I call and can get them to drive down Friday as soon as she gets out of school, then Eliot can tune the piano." She grimaced. "It won't hold, of course, but it ought to be all right for a dress rehearsal Saturday and a Sunday evening performance."

"What won't hold?"

"The pitch. Pianos that are tuned regularly hold their pitch much better. And I bet it's dry in here. Maybe I'll set a pan of water beneath it to increase the humidity a bit." She rose and picked up the cover, and Alice automatically moved to help her.

"Perhaps we should go home, and you can use the piano there."

"Good idea. Once I get the arrangements worked out, you and I can go over the script together."

As they left the sanctuary, Alice put an arm around Louise's waist. "There aren't words to express how much better I feel about this play already. Thank you so much, Louise."

Louise was looking out the front window again. It was Thursday afternoon, and the two sisters had begun to decorate the family Christmas tree as soon as Alice got home from work. Louise had spent the day completing her musical preparations for that evening's rehearsal of the Christmas show.

"Louise," Alice said with exaggerated patience. "What on earth are you looking at? That's the fourth time you've checked that window."

Louise dropped the lace curtain, shrugging as she turned around. "Nothing. I just enjoy the view. It's lovely to look out and see something so dear and familiar."

Moments later, Father entered the room. "This brings back memories," he said, blue eyes twinkling, as he regarded his daughters' decorating efforts.

Alice glanced up and smiled. "Hello, Father. How are the Simpsons?"

Father Howard had been out on pastoral calls, and Alice knew his last one had been to a woman in the congregation who was recovering from a bout of pneumonia.

"Florence is improving," her father reported. He wandered over to the couch, where Louise was unpacking treasured ornaments. He reached down and carefully held up an elongated glass teardrop painted in shades of gold, pink and burgundy. "This was one of your mother's favorite ornaments. It was part of a set of six I gave her the year we—"

A loud clunking on the front porch startled them.

"Are we expecting anyone?" Alice walked toward the entry, not waiting for an answer. She opened the door and saw a slender woman with a long dark braid struggling with a large suitcase. "Hello," she said. "May I help—*Jane!*" Alice didn't often squeal, but the sight of her younger sister's grinning countenance drew a shriek from her. "Father! Louise! Jane's here."

She rushed forward to clasp her younger sibling in a tight hug. "What are you doing here? You're two days early!"

Jane set down the suitcase with a *thunk* and opened her arms wide for Alice's embrace. "Shall I go away and come back then?"

"Don't you dare!"

Father carried in the forgotten suitcase and then turned to embrace his youngest child. Alice closed the door and announced, "This is *wonderful!* The whole family! Well, except for Eliot and Cynthia, but you know what I mean."

"We do." Louise nodded. "It's like old times." She enfolded her sister in her arms, as Father stepped back a pace. "Hello, dear. It's splendid to see you."

"I'm so glad you called," Jane said, returning the hug. She turned to Alice, as she stripped off her blue cape and tossed it over a chair. "Louise called on Saturday and told me she had decided to come home a few days early, so I thought I'd do the same. Couldn't let her outdo me for the 'good sister' award, right?"

"You *both* get the award," Alice proclaimed. "This is the best Christmas surprise I've ever had."

"Better than the red bike?" Louise asked.

Alice laughed. "That was pretty great. But this... this is better." Then her happiness dimmed a tiny bit. "Although I'm going to be so busy until Sunday, I won't have nearly as much time as I'd like to visit."

"Louise told me about your play. I figured I'd just tag along to rehearsals. Maybe I can help with costuming or the set or something."

Alice froze. *The set!* "Oh no," she groaned, sinking onto the arm of the couch. "Jane, there *is* no set. I completely forgot about it!"

Jane's eyes widened.

Louise clapped a hand to her forehead. "I should have mentioned it, but I assumed it wouldn't be in place until the dress rehearsal."

"Oh, this is terrible." Alice felt panic rising. "I can't possibly get a set together in time for the show on Sunday. We have rehearsal tonight. I have to work until three tomorrow and Saturday, and then our dress rehearsal starts at four on Saturday."

"That's great!" Jane said brightly.

Both of her elder sisters turned and looked at her. "Great?" They spoke in unison.

"It is," Jane insisted. "Louise is helping with the music, and we all know there's not a musical bone in my body. But I can create a set! I can watch tonight and make some notes on what we need."

We. Alice swallowed as she regarded her sisters, her eyes growing misty. Was there anyone on earth with better sisters?

A bit later, Alice was about to head up the stairs with fresh towels for Jane, when she noticed her father in the study.

Face glowing, she stuck her head around the door frame. "How long did you know about their coming?"

He smiled. "Not long at all. Louise called on Sunday and told me she was going to try to get away. Then when she arrived, she gave me the news about Jane."

"You're pretty good at keeping secrets."

He winked at her. Then he laid down the

fountain pen he'd been using and looked at her seriously. "I ran into Mrs. Rockwell at the Coffee Shop today. She is utterly thrilled that you are giving Celeste a large speaking role." He smiled at her. "You have a good heart. Celeste has needed this kind of self-esteem boost."

Alice stared at him, taken aback. "You knew Celeste has learning problems?"

He nodded. "Oh yes. Her parents worry about her."

"When I told you I had given her the lead, why didn't you tell me?"

"I didn't feel that I should influence your selection," he said. "This is an excellent opportunity for Celeste."

"That's what her mother said." Alice let her exasperation show. "But honestly, Father, that was the last complication I needed." She leveled a severe glance at him. "Thank heavens Louise is here. Please pray she has better luck than I pulling this show together."

Father's eyes sparkled, and he shot her a grin that was pure Jane. "I sincerely doubt Louise needs my prayers. I think we'd better pray that the children survive Hurricane Louise tonight."

When all had arrived at rehearsal that evening, Alice clapped her hands together. "Good evening, boys and girls." She turned and indicated her family members. "These are my sisters, Ms. Howard and Mrs. Smith. Tonight we're going to do a quick run-through. Then we'll sing all the songs before we do the whole play one more time. Mrs. Smith is going to watch, and she may have some suggestions for us. She's done many productions like this."

All the children found their places.

"All right. Let's get started."

Louise sat in silence as Alice's cast stumbled through the play. Once or twice when the Pfiffer-Trimble team got silly, Alice silenced them with nothing more than a raised eyebrow. Celeste seemed to be having a little less difficulty with her lines, although she still needed frequent prompting. Her singing, unfortunately, couldn't get enough help to make it sound good.

When they had finished, there was silence in the church. Then Louise rose to her feet and began to clap. Alice and Jane quickly followed suit.

The children beamed.

"Very nice work, boys and girls." Alice suspected Louise could easily be a very scary teacher, but her tone was gentle and admiring. "I see a few little things here and there I could suggest to improve it. Let me know if you're interested in hearing them—"

"We are!"

"Please, Mrs. Smith?"

Alice saw the hint of a smile playing around Louise's lips, and she realized her sister had deliberately led the group into asking for her advice.

Alice took a seat in a pew and watched as Louise guided the group through their music and then went through the play, changing what she called "blocking" to better showcase certain scenes, and reminding the children to speak their lines facing the audience even if the actor to whom they were speaking was standing "upstage," or behind them.

When Louise seemed satisfied that the children had absorbed her instructions, they started from the top and went through the whole show again. Alice watched in delight as her young actors seemed to swell with confidence and pride.

While the rehearsal went on, Jane sat in a pew

with a yellow pad and a pencil, scribbling notes. Alice took a deep breath. If Jane could come up with something simple, it would be fine—even if the audience might have to use an extra dollop of imagination.

As parents arrived to pick up their children, Alice stood near the door to bid everyone good-bye.

"Hello, Alice," Tina Carsten said as she entered. "How is the show coming? Kimmy refuses to tell me much about it. She says it's going to be a surprise."

Alice smiled. "Kimmy is quite an extraordinary young lady. I don't know what I'd have done without her."

Tina's face lit up. "Oh good! I know I annoy her sometimes insisting that she perform, but it's so important that she get over her tendency to hang back." Her expression sobered. "I don't ever want my children to suffer the teasing I did as a shy child." She smiled. "I'm sure that's hard to believe, but getting up in front of people terrified me so much that I stuttered badly." Her smile faded. "Children can be cruel, and I don't want Kimmy to go through anything like that. So thank you for everything you've done. I've never seen her so eager to come to a play rehearsal."

Tina moved past Alice then to collect Kimmy and depart. Alice winced, imagining how Tina was going to react when she learned on Sunday night that Kimmy didn't have the lead.

"Alice," Jane called out to her, "I have some questions about the set for you. Is this a good time?"

"The last child just left," Alice said. "Why don't we go home, put on our pajamas and talk about it over some tea and cookies?"

Louise approached, carrying Alice's coat as well as her own. "I think that's a good plan."

Alice turned out the lights, and the three sisters walked out into the bright moonlight. "I could hardly believe it was the same group of children after you got finished with them tonight!"

Louise smiled modestly. "You've done a very good job with them, dear. Really, all I did was work on the music and offer them some suggestions to polish their performances." She frowned. "Although your tone-deaf lead is a bit of a problem."

Alice sighed. "I know. I had no idea when I gave her the part that she couldn't sing."

"I may have a solution," Louise said. Then she shook a finger as Alice opened her mouth to inquire. "No, I'm not telling. You'll just have to wait until dress rehearsal on Saturday."

After work on Friday, Alice met Louise and Jane in front of Sylvia's Buttons, a business that had opened a few months earlier in Acorn Hill. Alice rarely had time to indulge in crafts, so she hadn't been in before, although she had met the owner, Sylvia Songer, at the Coffee Shop a few weeks ago.

Jane waved enthusiastically as Alice approached. "I made my list!"

"Your list?"

"I scrounged up almost everything around the house today, but there are a few things I need for the set."

They stepped into the little shop and saw that it was filled with bolts of holiday-themed fabrics, kits and supplies for various types of needle arts.

"Ooh." Jane looked around with a sigh. "This place must be heaven for people who like crafts."

"Hello, Alice." Sylvia stepped out from behind a curtain at the rear of the shop, a tape measure draped around her neck. She was a slim young woman with strawberry-blond hair and big dark eyes. Alice thought she seemed like a tiny, bright-eyed bird sometimes, with her quick movements and bursts of energy. "Nice to see you again."

"Hi, Sylvia. How are things going with your business?"

Sylvia smiled. "It was a bit slow in the beginning, but more and more people are coming in."

"That's wonderful." Alice was sincerely pleased that the community seemed to be supporting the fledgling business. "Sylvia, these are my sisters." She took a moment to introduce the women. "They're here for the holidays, and they're helping me with the musical at the church. Jane has a list of things she needs for our set."

Sylvia nodded, smiling at Jane. "Why don't we take a look and see what we can find?" The pair was soon immersed in a discussion of the best way to create a fake bush, leaving Alice and Louise to smile at each other.

"Calling Jane was a very smart move on my part," Louise opined, her blue eyes twinkling.

Alice laughed. "Indeed it was. If not for Jane, who knows when I would have realized I had no set."

Louise pointed at something right behind Alice. "Oh look. I might get one of those for Cynthia for Christmas. Aren't they gorgeous?"

Alice turned. Sylvia had a variety of handmade Christmas stockings displayed. Some hung from a cleverly constructed facade of a fireplace, while others were draped over a rocking chair and a basket and hung over quilt racks. Some of the stockings were cross-stitched masterpieces that must have taken years to complete. Others were appliquéd in various felt and fabric pieces and garnished with sequins and sparkling thread. Still others were prettily pieced and quilted in a variety of lovely Christmas-colored fabrics.

Alice decided she would get one for little Beth McCann. Most of the stockings had a space at the top. Maybe Sylvia would personalize it for her.

"Ah, you've noticed my stockings." Sylvia had left Jane's side.

Alice nodded. "They're stunning."

Sylvia nodded. "I design stockings every chance I get throughout the year. It's a hobby of mine. Are you interested in one in particular?"

"I need a stocking for a little girl," Alice told her. "Do you add names to them?"

Sylvia nodded. "It's a free service when you buy one."

A second thought struck. "Actually, I'd like three."

"And I must have one as well," Louise declared.

Sylvia pointed at a display against the far wall. "Those are some of my personal favorites. I think they'll go fast, so if you see something you like, you'd better grab it now."

Alice and Louise approached the display. These stockings were appliquéd in a wide range of fabrics and sparkly embellishments. A charming little angel done in shades of blue, cream and gold caught her eye. That one had to be for Beth.

Her gaze traveled over the others. A Christmas tree with gifts piled beneath it was simply beautiful. Liz would love it. And for Suzy...ah, there. A jolly Santa waved from his sleigh as it spiraled through a deep midnight-blue sky studded with sparkling sequin stars.

"Alice, look at this!" Louise held a stocking in her hand. "It's perfect!"

Alice inspected it. "Oh goodness. How lovely." The stocking was a work of art. A fireplace mantel held two hanging stockings, while a merry fire leaped in the hearth and a pretty tabby cat curled on a rug before it. Tiny angels embroidered in iridescent thread flitted above the stockings, carefully dropping small gifts into them. "My daughter Cynthia loves angels!" Louise told Sylvia.

"These are stunning," Alice said. "How can you bear to part with them?"

Sylvia smiled. "It's not quite so hard when you know they're going to be treasured. I can tell from your faces how excited you are."

"Indeed we are!" Louise marched over to the counter. "I'd like the name Cynthia put on this one."

⌒

"I have one more stop to make before dinner," Alice told her sisters. "Shall I drop you off at the house first?" Louise and Jane had opted to walk into town, wanting to soak up as much of their home visit as possible.

"If you'd like company, we could go along," Jane suggested.

Alice pointed to her car. "Climb in."

"And after we eat, we're all going over to the church to put this set together," Jane decreed. "I'm going to need every pair of hands in this family."

A few minutes later, Alice parked in front of Suzy McCann's home.

"Hello, Alice. What a nice surprise." Suzy smiled as she stood in the doorway of her small home.

"I should have called," Alice told her.

"No, no. I love surprises. Hello," she said to Jane and Louise, as she motioned for them to enter, and Alice closed the chilly winter air out. "I'm Suzy. Consider your hands shaken."

The sisters laughed.

"We're Alice's sisters. I'm Louise."

"And I'm Jane."

"Where's your mother?" Alice asked Suzy. "I heard your casts clunking against the door when you tried to open it."

"I didn't just try, I did open it." Suzy grinned. "It takes me awhile to get things done, but I'm managing. With the simple things, at least. Changing a diaper is beyond me right now."

"And you're complaining?" Alice winked.

Suzy laughed. She indicated the couch. "Have a seat. Mom just walked to the corner store, and Beth's napping."

"We can't stay." Alice held up the bag from Sylvia's. "I just wanted to drop these off." She offered it to Suzy, then realized that wasn't going to work.

Their eyes met, and they exchanged a wry smile. "Sorry," Alice said. "I'll do the honors." She reached into the bag and pulled out the angel stocking first. "A little something for Beth."

Suzy's eyes widened and almost immediately filled with tears. "Oh, Alice," she whispered. "That is absolutely precious."

"I saw it and just knew that little angel belonged to your daughter."

Suzy smiled, despite her swimming eyes. "Those two things aren't always synonymous these days."

"No one's at her best with chicken pox," Alice said.

Louise's eyes widened in sympathy. "Your daughter has chicken pox? My daughter Cynthia had them as a toddler too. I'm not sure who was more miserable, she or I."

"Yes, but I had them when I was sixteen," Jane reminded her. "Trust me, when your little one is sixteen, she will be *thrilled* that she's already had chicken pox. I missed Homecoming that year," she added in an aggrieved tone.

"I'd forgotten that," mused Louise.

"You'd already moved away," Jane said. "Alice was the one who took care of me."

"Alice is very good at doing that," Suzy said.

Uncomfortable with the praise, Alice reached into the bag and drew out the two remaining stockings. She held them up for Suzy's inspection. "Merry Christmas. This one is yours"—she tilted her head toward the one on the right featuring Santa Claus— "and this one is your mom's." She indicated the Christmas tree.

"Oh, Alice," Suzy said, "you really shouldn't have. But aren't they gorgeous?" She raised one arm and awkwardly ran a finger over the beadwork on the sleigh. "Thank you so much!"

She began to move forward to hug Alice but checked the motion. "This is driving me *crazy*!" she moaned, indicating her casts, her vivacious expression dimming. "I can't do *anything*."

"It's only temporary," Alice soothed. "Those casts will be gone before you know it."

"Not until after Christmas," Suzy said glumly. "I can't even surprise Mom with a Christmas gift because she's going to have to come with me to buy it!"

Jane's expression sharpened. "Would you like a little help?"

Suzy stared at her. "Pardon?"

"Oh, Jane, that's a great idea," Alice said. "I have to work tomorrow, but you're free." She turned to Suzy. "Why don't you let Jane take you shopping?"

"I couldn't impose on you like that," Suzy said, shaking her head.

"Shopping is never an imposition for me. I'd love to take you. Now what time shall I pick you up?"

❧

As the sisters got out of the car at home, the sound of a car pulling into the driveway drew their attention. The rear window rolled down as they turned to look at it. A head with long dark hair whipping in the breeze appeared in the window. "Hi, Mom! Aunt Alice! Aunt Jane! We're here."

Louise clasped her hands together, a smile lighting up her features. "Cynthia and Eliot!" Almost immediately, she frowned and glanced at her watch. "They're early. I hope he didn't speed."

"Hello, dear," Alice called to Louise's twelve-year-old daughter, as she and Jane both started across the lawn.

As the two members of the Smith family emerged from the car, Cynthia rushed into Alice's embrace, while Jane hugged Louise's husband Eliot. "Oh, it's so good to see you both," she said. "How on earth did I let a whole year go by without coming home?"

"I don't know," Alice answered the rhetorical question. "But I promise I'm going to make more of an effort to see more of all of you. As soon as these holidays are over, I'm checking my calendar to make plans to vacation in Philadelphia *and* California next year."

"Ooh, can I come to California with you, Aunt Alice?" Cynthia asked.

"That's a terrific idea." Jane nodded approvingly. "Maybe all five of you could come out for a visit."

"That's a lovely idea." Louise grabbed a suitcase and headed for the house. "But right now, I vote we all go inside out of this cold. Father," she called as she threw open the door, "Cynthia and Eliot are here."

Father came from the direction of his study, as they all spilled into the entryway. He enveloped his only grandchild in a tight hug before clasping hands with Eliot. "Just in time for dinner," he said, smiling. "How have you been?"

Jane and Alice got supper ready while Louise helped her family settle in.

Soon everyone gathered around the large old table

where a platter of sliced ham and bowls of Alice's home-baked macaroni and cheese, green beans and fruit salad awaited the hungry family.

All clasped hands and bowed their heads as Father offered a prayer. "Dear heavenly Father, we thank You for bringing each member of our family to the table this evening. Thank You for the bonds of love we share despite the miles that so often stand between us. Bless this food and the hands that prepared it. In Your name we pray. Amen."

"Amen," everyone murmured.

"And dear God, please especially help us to support Alice as she prepares for the Christmas musical," Jane added.

"Amen!" Alice said with a laugh.

◦

Dinner ended, and everyone helped to tidy the kitchen.

As Alice put the last plate away, Jane said, "All right. Let's get our coats."

"Where are we going?" Cynthia looked pleased at the prospect of an excursion.

"All of us," Jane said, "are going over to the chapel

for a decorating session. I have a set design in mind, and it's not complicated, but I need willing hands."

"Mine are willing." Alice held them up and waggled her fingers.

Cynthia giggled. "Mine too."

Louise turned toward Alice, her dark hair gleaming in the light, and Alice noticed the first strands of silver in it. "Eliot was going to tune the piano first thing in the morning, but if we're all going to be at the chapel, he might as well tune it now."

"You'll have to keep the chatter down to a dull roar," her husband told them.

Father smiled. "I suppose if all of you are going, I should come along. Surely there's some way I can help."

"Absolutely!" Jane practically radiated energy. "I need help with painting and carpentry, as well as decorating-type things."

They donned their coats and picked up bags and boxes of supplies that Jane had gathered. At the chapel, they set the items on the front row pews.

Eliot went immediately to the piano. When he drew off the dust cover and hit the keys, his reaction was so like Louise's that Alice had to laugh.

"Wow." Cynthia covered her ears. "That's hideous, Dad. Stop."

"Can't," Eliot said cheerfully. "At least, not entirely." He opened a small bag and laid out several tools. Then he opened the top of the piano to expose the hammers and strings.

"All right, troops," Jane announced, "Here's what I want to do...." She had created a set using a refrigerator box she had scavenged from somewhere. Opened and flattened, she planned to paint one side with an interior scene and the other with an outside view of a park. Behind it, she wanted to hang a large sheet painted with a view of a neighborhood street. When the interior scene was positioned squarely in the middle of the altar, which was serving as their stage, only a bit of the backdrop could be seen through the window and door in the house. But when the action shifted to the park, the backdrop moved to one side and the refrigerator-box-set to the other, doubling the vista. It was an extremely clever design.

"I would never have been able to come up with something like this," Alice said. Then her face fell. "Are we really going to be able to make this in one evening?"

"Of course we are," Jane said. "Cynthia, why don't

you start crumpling sheets of newspaper into balls. We're going to fasten them to a box and then spray-paint the whole thing to resemble a bush. Dad, I need you to build me two identical supports that look like this." She paused and handed him an illustration. "They're really easy, just triangles with two supports to hold them upright. That's what we'll use to hold up the refrigerator box."

"But what if someone bumps it?" Cynthia asked.

"Smart cookie," Jane said approvingly. She held up a package of hook-and-eye latches. "We'll put one hook on each triangle side that's standing up. Then we'll fasten eyes on both sides of the cardboard. When we turn the set, it'll be easy to hook them together so they can't accidentally be knocked over."

"Smart cookie," Cynthia said, grinning.

Jane grabbed her and rubbed her knuckles across the top of Cynthia's head. To Louise, she said, "When did your daughter become a smart aleck?"

"I get it from Dad," Cynthia informed her. "When Mom's on a tear, Dad says the only way to handle her is to make her laugh."

There was a muffled snort of laughter from the direction of the piano.

"Well, I never!" Louise tried to look put out, but she couldn't quite manage it with Alice and Father both guffawing.

Jane cleared her throat. "Moving on," she said, "Alice, you and I are going to paint that sheet."

"Oh boy," Alice said. "You do recall that my talents run to stick figures, right?"

"It doesn't need to be perfect," Jane said. "While we're doing that, I have another job for you, Louise." She handed her eldest sister a sheet of paper. "These items need to be hidden behind the altar in this arrangement."

"I presume that's a backdrop." Louise turned and eyed the "stage." "How are you going to hang it?"

Jane hesitated. "I haven't worked that out yet," she admitted.

"We have a pair of iron uprights in storage downstairs," Father said. "We've tied lines to them in the past to hang children's artwork to dry. We could hang the backdrop from a line between the two."

Eliot laid down a tuning fork. "I'll give you a hand bringing them up," he said to Father.

The three sisters and Cynthia were hard at work when the men returned, and soon everyone was engrossed in his own task. Alice painted trees on the sheet. Louise helped Cynthia finish the bush, and Jane took it outside for a quick coat of spray-paint. Then Alice surrendered her paintbrush to Cynthia and went to hold the lengths of two-by-four that Father had cut, while he nailed them together.

It was nearly eleven by the time they were finished. "Oh, Jane, our set looks terrific," Alice said when they all stood at the back of the sanctuary to view their efforts.

"I haven't had this much fun in years!" Jane exclaimed.

Louise smiled, reaching for each of her sisters' hands and squeezing. "It's good to be with you both."

"I agree." Jane nodded. Alice just smiled happily.

❧

Louise, Eliot, Cynthia and Jane all accompanied Alice to the final dress rehearsal on Saturday afternoon. As they walked over to the chapel, Alice sent up a silent prayer of thanks. *Lord, thank You so much for my family, for their willingness to pitch in and use their talents in Your service, for their support and love.*

Louise ran the rehearsal as she and Alice had agreed. Alice was delighted that the children didn't seem to question the change of leadership. Then again, they all were so obviously wowed by the set that they were unusually attentive, everyone remembering his stage directions and handling assignments to move props as needed.

First, they did a simple run-through of the staging so everyone knew what his tasks were. Then it was time for a full dress rehearsal. Fortunately, with the contemporary setting, there was little need for costuming.

Alice, Eliot and Jane sat in a pew to watch the transformation. Cynthia had volunteered to be the prompter, and she was seated on a stool behind the backdrop, where the audience couldn't hear her but the actors could, if someone needed a line.

The dress rehearsal went smoothly. Celeste was markedly more capable with her lines. When the young girl prepared for her solo, however, Alice grabbed Jane's hand. Celeste opened her mouth and began to sing—and Alice did a double-take. "Celeste is singing the melody. Do you hear that?"

Jane shrugged. "I didn't even notice that she sounded bad before."

"Trust me, she did," Alice whispered. "I wonder why she's suddenly doing so much better."

Eliot leaned close and spoke into Alice's ear. "Louise had an idea," he told Alice. "Often people who can't carry a tune can do better when they hear another strong voice next to them. It's when they have no guidance that they sound the most off-key."

"Cynthia's singing along from behind her, isn't she?" Alice was truly shocked at the difference in Celeste's ability. "Eliot, did I ever tell you what an amazing woman you married?"

Eliot sent her a beaming smile. "I think of that every day," he said. Returning his gaze to his wife, he watched her at the piano with such love in his eyes that Alice felt her own heart melt. *Thank You, God,* she thought, *for this wonderful man who so cherishes my sister.*

The following evening, Alice and Eliot were seated near the front of the chapel beside Rev. Howard, while Louise had taken a seat at the newly tuned piano. Cynthia was in her hidden prompter's place behind the backdrop. Suddenly, Alice realized Jane was missing. She glanced around but didn't see her sister.

The set looked terrific. Arranged for the opening scene in a family living room, a wing chair, borrowed from her father's office, and a piecrust table from the same source were set to one side, with an oval rug and two chairs from the Sunday school area on the other. The walls were painted an oatmeal hue with pale blue stripes to simulate wallpaper, and Jane had even placed her own surprisingly realistic-looking painting in an ornate frame on the wall beside the door.

All around her, Alice could hear ripples of excited whispering. She spotted Tina Carsten sitting near the front. Alice wondered if Kimmy had told her anything about the show. She probably should brace herself for an earful when the performance ended.

Then she spotted Jane, coming up the aisle with Liz Henshaw, Suzy McCann and little Beth, who clearly had recovered from her bout with chicken pox. Oh, it was so like Jane, bless her, to remember her new friend. Jane paused beside their pew. Rev. Howard stepped out and the rest all obligingly slid down to make room for the newcomers.

Then Rev. Howard walked to the front. "Ladies and gentlemen," he said, "welcome to Grace Chapel. For a number of years, it has been a tradition for our congregation's children to produce a short musical to celebrate the true meaning of the season. This year's show does that. Titled *Big Hearts in Tough Times,* the play features a pair of sisters played by Celeste Rockwell and Ellen Sizemore."

Alice saw Tina Carsten start in her seat, as if she'd been stung by a bee.

Her father continued. "Each sister wants to do something special for her sibling for Christmas. But without any money, how can each of them make that happen?" He smiled. "It's a great little story, and what makes this one even more special is that it was written—every single word of it—by a young lady right here in our congregation. Miss Kimmy Carsten is our playwright. Let's give her a hand." He began to clap enthusiastically, and the congregation followed suit. The children pushed Kimmy to the front of the group so that those seated in the church could see her if they turned around.

Blushing scarlet, she gave them a wide, delighted grin before stepping back into place again. Alice would bet her last cent that Kimmy had never looked that delighted with a major role in a play. She hoped Tina would be able to accept that her daughter's talent might take a different path than her own.

"And there's one more person we need to thank,"

her father continued. "My daughter Alice stepped into the director's shoes when Cathy Carling's mother suffered a stroke, and Cathy needed to go to her bedside. Alice has no music or theater background, so this has been quite a challenging experience for her. I would personally like to thank her for taking on this task when she would have had a perfectly sound reason not to do so." He smiled over the heads between them, and she felt tears sting her eyes at the pride and love showing in his. "Thank you, Alice."

Too touched to speak, she nodded her head.

"Without further delay, I'm proud to present *Big Hearts in Tough Times*."

As Louise began to play a prelude composed of the songs used in the show, the first child started up the aisle to the "stage." Louise let the music fade as the last child took his place, and Celeste spoke her first lines: "I love my little sister. That's how this whole story began...."

Alice watched closely as the sisters demonstrated their affection for each other. The first musical number was "Here We Come A-Caroling," as the young actors sang for their neighbors. It went well, and then the second scene followed, in which the younger sister thought in vain of things she could do for her older sister for Christmas. Celeste was managing her lines admirably.

In scene three, the children's mother sang the first verse of "All Through the Night," after which a choir of angels joined her for two more verses.

The production wound its way to the conclusion. The younger sister had purchased two concert tickets for her big sister by using the money she had been saving up for a new bicycle. The older sister, in turn, had promised a month of babysitting services to a neighbor in exchange for the money to purchase a bike helmet and other accessories to surprise her little sister. One of the babysitting dates, of course, was the night of the concert. In the end, they sold the concert tickets and donated the money and biking items to a foundation for underprivileged children. Then came the closing number, "Let There Be Peace on Earth." Celeste had a moment's nervous hesitation when her solo music began, but Alice could tell the instant she heard Cynthia's voice backing her up. The child's entire demeanor changed, confidence squaring her shoulders as she managed a passably on-key rendition of the first verse.

When the play ended to thunderous applause, Alice wondered if it would be possible for her to run away before Tina Carsten could track her down. But no. She was trapped by Celeste Rockwell's mother and father, both of whom had tears in their eyes. Mrs. Rockwell grabbed her and hugged until Alice gasped for breath.

"Thank you so much," she cried. "You can't imagine what this experience has done for Celeste."

After a moment, Alice was swept off to another group where she found Liz Henshaw and the McCanns. "That was incredible!" Suzy's eyes were shining. "I don't know how you made time for us with everything else you had going on, but we're very grateful that you did. Merry Christmas, Alice."

"Merry Christmas to you too."

"We brought candy apples for the actors," Suzy said. "Jane took them downstairs so the children could take one as they left the room. Make sure you get one too." She grinned. "I even helped stir a little bit."

Then Tina Carsten approached. Alice braced herself for the blast.

"Alice." Tina's voice was uncharacteristically quiet. "I owe you an apology. It seems you know my daughter better than I do."

"Oh no, I—"

"Oh yes," Tina said. "Thank you for recognizing her talents."

"You're welcome." Alice knew she sounded surprised, but it didn't matter because Tina already had moved away.

Other parents thanked her, congratulated her, tried to recruit her for various activities. She tactfully declined.

Then the older girls who had been in the play approached. Celeste held out a small gift box.

"This is for you," Celeste said.

Realizing they expected her to open it, Alice carefully pulled the little box apart to reveal a lovely little hand-carved angel ornament in a pretty red-toned wood that she thought might be cherry. "Thank you," Kimmy said, "for being our angel and helping us to have a play without Miss Carling this year."

Alice smiled. "You're most welcome."

"But Miss Howard, we don't want it to end," Celeste went on. "We like doing things with you, and we'd like you to keep meeting with us. Kimmy and I want to do special things for others—"

"Sort of like a service club," Kimmy inserted.

"Yeah," Celeste confirmed. "We'd like you to help us start something like that."

Alice was surprised but not speechless. "Girls," she said, "I'm very honored by your request. I would love to keep working with you."

"Hey!" Ellen said. "I know. We can be the Angels!"

"The name of our group has to stand for something," Julia objected.

Hastily, Alice said, "I'll tell you what. Early in January, we can meet and discuss this a little more. In the meantime, perhaps you could brainstorm a bit and come up with some possible names for the group."

"I want to be an Angel," Ellen said stubbornly.

"Maybe," Kimmy told her, "we can make that stand for something special. It's called an acronym. You know, like SWAK stands for 'sealed with a kiss'?"

"It'll have to be something as special as all of you." Alice hugged each girl in turn. "Have a wonderful Christmas. I'll see you soon."

She turned, as her own family approached. "I am humbled," said Father Howard, "by the grace of a God Who gave me three such amazing daughters, a talented son-in-law and a granddaughter with such a giving heart. Thank you all for your contributions to tonight's program. Alice, I especially appreciate all your hard work. Like the sisters in Kimmy's script, you didn't think about what was in it for you. You were determined to do it because it was important to others."

Alice smiled and put her hand through her father's arm. "Christmas is about giving. I gave some time"—she grinned—"and maybe a little sleep, but I got to spend some wonderfully memorable hours with my family."

$\mathcal{I}$ can see why that memory is so special to you," Jane said softly. She set down her cider and rose from the couch to touch the little wooden angel hanging on the tree.

"That's the ornament the children gave me after the play," Alice said.

"I remember. You were wonderful with them," Jane said.

"It was amazing how the play came together. I had no idea what I was doing."

"You seemed a bit frazzled." Jane chuckled and returned to her seat. "But didn't we have a great time?"

"Yes. After the cavalry arrived. I couldn't have done it without you two and Cynthia." Alice shook her head.

"And Eliot," Louise added. "Tuning that piano…"

She rolled her eyes. "I've never heard a piano so discordant. I was afraid he wouldn't be able to fix it, but he worked his magic."

"Father helped too, but you had it well in hand when we arrived. We just helped with finishing touches," Jane said.

"Touches?" Alice laughed out loud. "The boys were out of control. The singing was a disaster. I had no sets."

"Yes, but look what came out of it. The beginning of the ANGELs," Louise said. "What a wonderful group, Alice. And how amazing that it's endured for more than two decades!"

"Goodness. It's hard to believe it was that long ago," Jane said. "Those were good times, when we were all together."

"Wonderful times, in spite of the challenges," Alice said. "God turned that misfortune into a blessing for me. I loved how our family worked together to make the Christmas musical a success, and I love working with the ANGELs. That wouldn't have happened if Cathy Carling's poor mother hadn't had a stroke."

"She recovered fully, though, didn't she?" Jane asked.

"Yes, thank the Lord," Alice said, remembering how relieved Cathy was when physical therapy worked wonders on her mother. "So what about you, Jane? Which Christmas stands out to you?"

"Hmmm. Let me think." Jane flipped her long dark hair over her shoulder and leaned back on the couch. "I have so many special memories....I always loved Father's stories about the first Christmas. He made the wonder of the Christ child come alive, and I loved that." She smiled at her sisters. "And you two made Christmas a magical time for me. But one of my favorite Christmases happened after we started the inn. I remember that year was especially cold."

Jane gazed at the candles and decorations on the mantel. She'd decorated with bayberry candles and greens that year too.

"Do you remember, Alice?"

Alice nodded. It was several years earlier, just after Father had passed away and Jane and Louise had moved home to open Grace Chapel Inn.

"We were at church two weeks before Christmas, and I asked you about Hazel Tucker," Jane said. "I hadn't seen her since I moved home. I thought maybe she had died. I was surprised when you said she was still living in her house, but she didn't get out. She was ancient when she taught my Sunday school class."

Louise laughed. "Hardly ancient. Elderly, perhaps."

Jane smiled a bit ruefully. "Shows how our perspective changes as we grow older. I remember thinking I wanted to do something nice for her. Then I noticed other people were missing. Like my dance teacher, Evelyn Potter. Same thing. A whole generation had gotten old and feeble while I was away."

"I remember," Alice said. "And I could see the wheels spinning in your head, cooking up a plan."

Jane laughed. "What else would I do? The kitchen is my studio."

"A fact that delights us daily," Louise said. "I didn't recall how it started, but I remember that year as the Cookie Christmas."

Jane's Christmas Memory

*L*ess than two weeks before Christmas, Grace Chapel Inn was almost ready for the holidays. The outdoor lights decorated the roof lines of the stately Victorian home, and illuminated wreaths were hung in the windows. Colored lights twinkled brightly from the tall Christmas tree that filled the living room's bay window.

Jane was in the living room decorating the mantel. She laid down fresh pine boughs, then artfully nestled dried hydrangea blooms and holly sprigs among the branches, leaving the center bare.

On each side of the arrangement, she set a red bayberry pillar candle, and then hung glittery crocheted snowflakes on red satin ribbons from the mantel. Stepping back, she studied her work with a critical eye. The snowflakes had just enough sparkle to reflect the light from the living room chandelier as they swayed gently from the warmth of the fire. She scattered a few flakes of Epsom salts on the boughs, giving them a frosted appearance.

"Lovely!" Alice exclaimed, entering the room carrying a well-worn cardboard box.

At Alice's voice, Wendell, their gray-striped tabby cat, opened one eye, then stretched his white paws, let out a yawn and turned over on the couch.

"Wendell's unimpressed, but thanks." Jane gathered up her supplies. "Oh, you have the crèche. I left the place of honor for it on the mantel."

Jane took her supplies to the kitchen, then returned to watch Alice unpack the old, hand-painted papier-mâché nativity set.

Alice lovingly unwrapped the tissue paper around a piece, then handed it to Jane. The paint on the shepherd was chipped in spots, but to Jane that made it special. The old set had belonged to Grandmother Berry, and then to their mother. It always held an honored spot in their decorations, reminding them of the true reason they celebrated Christmas: their Savior's birth. Jane helped Alice arrange the stable with Mary and Joseph inside and the empty manger in the center. They always saved the baby Jesus figure until Christmas Day.

"Now it's perfect," Jane said as Alice placed a lamb next to the shepherd.

"I like the snowflakes," Alice said, placing the empty tissue paper in the old box. "Do you want to hang the stockings this year?"

"I thought we'd hang them from the mantel in the parlor."

"I'll bring them down when I put this box away," Alice said, heading up the stairs toward the attic.

"I'll make tea," Jane called after her. Then she peeked into the parlor where Louise was practicing a baroque arrangement of "Joy to the World." Jane loved hearing Louise play. Her sister had a magic touch on the piano.

Louise's beautiful Hummel nativity set had replaced the porcelain doll collection on the antique carved walnut table for the Christmas season.

Louise glanced up and paused, her foot pedal holding out the notes.

"Cup of tea?" Jane asked. "I've made date bread."

Louise nodded in time to the music. "As soon as I finish this movement," she said.

Jane backed out and shut the door. Jane hummed the modern version of the carol as she returned to the kitchen and turned on the burner beneath the kettle. She arranged slices of the warm bread on a plate with a small bowl of cream cheese and got out cups and saucers.

Alice came in just as the kettle whistled. She carried cream and sugar to the kitchen table. "Working on menus?" she asked, indicating the open cookbook and notebook on the table.

"I'm trying to decide which Christmas goodies to make this year."

"Whatever you make will be delicious. We don't have guests next week, you remember."

"I know. Much as I love cooking for guests, I'm looking forward to our own family Christmas. I've been thinking, since I'll have extra time, I'd like to hold a cookie drive for the shut-ins in town, like Evelyn Potter."

"That would be nice," Louise said as she came into the kitchen. "I know Evelyn has a caregiver who comes in to help her, and she gets meals delivered, so she has some company. But a little extra attention would be welcome, I'm sure. I can think of several people who'd like a visit."

"Ellen Moore is recovering from a knee

replacement. I know the Helping Hands ministry has taken meals to her, but I'm sure she'd like a holiday visit," Alice said. "I won't offer to bake cookies, but I'll be glad to help."

"Oh yoo-hoo!" called a shrill voice from outside the back door. The knob turned and Ethel walked in.

"Hello, Aunt Ethel," Jane said, standing. "Come sit and have a cup of tea. I made date bread."

Ethel closed her eyes and sniffed the air. "Heavenly. I shouldn't. I had a late lunch with Lloyd." Aunt Ethel had moved into the carriage house next to the inn after her husband passed away many years before. Now she was dating Lloyd Tynan, the mayor of Acorn Hill. She took a seat and reached for a piece of the moist dark bread.

Jane set a small plate and a cup and saucer in front of her, and then poured the tea. "And how is our mayor today?"

"Grumpy," Ethel said, then laughed. "He has so much on his mind, with the Christmas season in full swing downtown."

"Jane was just telling us she's planning a cookie drive for Acorn Hill's shut-ins for Christmas," Alice said.

"What a lovely idea. I'll be happy to donate some cookies."

"Thanks, Auntie. You're my first commitment," Jane said.

"When do you plan to hold this cookie drive?" Louise asked as she spread cream cheese on her date bread.

"I thought we could have a little party here on the twenty-second and ask all the guests to bring cookies. We can provide hot drinks and some hors d'oeuvres and sample some of the cookies, then divide the rest onto plates. After a little fellowship, we can split into groups to deliver the goody plates. How does that sound?"

"Wonderful. The ladies at church will all be happy to help," Ethel said.

"Oh. That's great, but I'd like to make it more of a community effort," Jane said. She could envision Aunt Ethel turning the idea into a major church outreach program. Aunt Ethel's heart was in the right place, but Jane had a simpler plan in mind.

After the last inn guests had finished breakfast, Jane cleared the rolls and muffins and the caddy of jams off the dining room table. Louise gathered up the soiled dishes to carry to the kitchen. Alice had left early for her shift at the hospital.

"Are you going to make a gingerbread house this year?" Louise asked.

Jane eyed the top of the buffet in the dining room where she usually put a gingerbread house and church scene. "I don't know. Maybe this year I'll do something different."

"Really? Like what?"

"I'm still thinking about it." Jane gave her sister a mysterious smile.

"You always come up with something imaginative, so I know it'll be worth waiting for."

Jane was considering a cookie nativity scene to go along with her cookie drive. After the dishes were done and Louise had gone to run errands and meet a friend in Potterston, Jane got out her cookie cutters. Digging through the box, she picked out an angel and some animals. She would have to make the other figures she needed.

She used her sketchpad to draw nativity figures,

basing her scale on a two-inch sheep cookie cutter. She sketched two shepherds, the wise men, Joseph and Mary and a manger with baby Jesus. Then she took a ball of twine and stretched out the string around each figure to calculate how much metal she would need for the cookie cutters. Armed with her totals, she grabbed her jacket and purse and headed out the back door.

Fred's Hardware Store buzzed with activity. The aisle of Christmas merchandise was filled with customers. Fred came out of the back carrying a long box with a picture of a perfect Christmas tree on the side. He took it up to the counter, where a man had a pile of ornaments and packages of lights.

"Morning, Jane, how are you?" Fred called out to her.

"I'm well. Looks like you're really busy."

"We're running an early sale on all the Christmas stuff. Need some artificial greens or a tree? We've got some bargains."

"No thanks, but I do need some craft supplies." Fred kept a good stock of things for do-it-yourselfers.

Jane usually knew just where to look for her items, but this time she needed handyman supplies. She headed toward the back.

"I'm looking for strips of copper and small clamps."

"I think we can find that back with building supplies," Fred said. "Do you need some work done at your home? I can come help."

"Oh thank you, Fred, but I'm making cookie cutters."

He gave her a puzzled look.

Jane laughed. "I'm making shapes to cut out cookie dough."

"Oh," he said, but he still looked confused.

With Fred's help she found a roll of one-inch copper that was pliable but heavy enough to hold a shape. She bought miniclamps with vinyl grips and a package of food-safe glue.

When Jane got home, she covered the kitchen table with newspaper, then spread out her materials. She cut lengths of the copper for each cookie cutter. Working carefully, she shaped the copper strips around the outline of each sketch, overlapping the ends and gluing them, then clamping the ends together until they set.

When she finished, Jane arranged the cookie cutters into a mock-up of her nativity scene. She smiled. It would work very well.

Next Jane mixed batches of gingerbread and sugar-cookie dough for her nativity scene and put them into the refrigerator, wrapped in plastic, to chill. She knew Louise's plans would keep her in Potterston for a couple of hours more, so that gave Jane time to work on Christmas presents. She went up to her third-floor bedroom and got out her supplies. She'd never done quilling before, but she'd decided to try this unique papercraft on gifts for her sisters. It didn't look difficult. You simply wound narrow strips of paper into coils and used them to create interesting decorative shapes. She had ordered two sepia-toned copies of an old photograph of Louise and Alice with her at her high school graduation, and she planned to frame them both with a border of filigreed paper quills to make them special. She had better get started.

~

A week before the cookie swap, Jane stepped into the warmth of Clarissa Cottrell's Good Apple bakery. This morning every table was occupied. The frigid temperatures outside no doubt encouraged people to linger. Carlene Moss sat at a table alone. She smiled and beckoned to Jane to join her.

"Good morning. What's new?"

"I was going to ask you," Carlene said. She was always on the lookout for a story for the *Acorn Nutshell*, which she edited and published. "You're out and about early. No guests at the inn?"

"Not until after Christmas. I thought I'd get out early and run errands."

"I hear you're starting a community project."

"I'm what?"

"I heard from the mayor that you are planning a community cookie drive. I can help you spread the word if you give me the basics so I can run a story this week. 'Tis the season, you know."

"Oh dear. Carlene, I have no intention of doing anything on such a grand scale." Jane shook her head. She guessed the source of the rumor was dear Aunt Ethel, bless her gossipy soul. Naturally, she told her special friend Lloyd Tynan, the mayor. And naturally he wanted to see it involve the whole community. He always looked for ways to promote community spirit. Not that Acorn Hill needed any help in that area.

Jane leaned toward Carlene and lowered her voice. "I want to keep this low-key. Just a small group of friends getting together to deliver some goodies to a few shut-ins in the area."

"Ah." Carlene laughed out loud. "You'd better tell the mayor before he puts up banners announcing the cookie drive."

Jane shuddered. "Thanks. I will." She gazed at her friend. It was one of those moments that made Jane realize how blessed she was. Carlene was single, like her, but she didn't have family around. "Would you like to join us? I'm asking a few friends to bring two dozen cookies. We'll divide them up and deliver them to people who can't get out. So far, I've only discussed this with my sisters, and, of course, Aunt Ethel."

Carlene smiled. "Now I understand where the mayor got his facts. I'd love to join you. When?"

"The twenty-second. Six o'clock. And I'll have hors d'oeuvres, in case you don't have time for dinner."

"Sounds like great fun. Thanks for including me. Now I'd better go to work and let you get on with your day." Carlene stood and slipped her arms into the sleeves of her down jacket.

"Squash any more rumors you hear, please," Jane said.

Carlene grinned. "You bet."

Lloyd was in the corner eating a doughnut, even though he was supposed to watch his diet. Ethel worried about him and his love of sweets. He looked up and Jane read the guilt on his face as she approached him.

"Don't tell your aunt," he said as she sat across from him.

"Good morning to you too," she said, with a laugh. "And I won't, if you do me a favor."

His shoulders relaxed. "I'm sorry. Good morning, Jane. Sure. Anything. What can I do for you?"

"I need you to stop a rumor. Evidently you've gotten the mistaken impression that I'm planning a community cookie drive."

"Oh. Yes. Your aunt mentioned something to me about it. You're not?"

"No. I'm not. I'm afraid Aunt Ethel has gotten a bit overly enthusiastic about my plan."

Lloyd nodded sagely. "I don't suppose you'd consider expanding to a community event. People love a good cause, especially at Christmastime."

"Sorry to disappoint you, but no. We don't have that much need. Acorn Hill does a great job of taking care of our own people. This is just a small gesture to bring a little Christmas cheer to those who can't get out."

"But..."

"I'd love to have you join us and help deliver the goodies. You know how much people love a personal visit from their mayor."

Lloyd inhaled, puffing out his chest. "You know I'll be happy to help any way I can. I don't bake, though."

Jane smiled. "That's all right. I'm sure we'll have plenty of cookies. Thanks. I knew I could count on you."

⌒

A cold blast of night air hit the side of Jane's face at the same time the moist heat of the oven whooshed out and warmed her.

"Yum. It smells like gingerbread in here." Alice shut the door, cutting off the cold. She shrugged off her wool jacket and hung it on a hook by the door.

Jane pulled a pan of cookies out of the oven and

set it on the counter. The rich, spicy scent of ginger and vanilla filled the kitchen. "This is for my cookie display, but I made extras. Water's hot. Would you like a cup of tea?"

"I could use a cup. It must be in the teens out there." Alice rubbed her hands together. Jane handed her a hot mug of tea. Alice wrapped her hands around the cup. "*Ahhh.*"

"How was the church board meeting? Anything exciting going on?"

"It was all right. Just routine."

Louise came through the door. "I just heard the weatherman predict this cold spell will last the rest of the month. He said it might climb up to the twenties by the end of the week."

"I hope it snows. I love a white Christmas. Join us for tea," Jane said. She scooped several cookies onto a plate.

"That's why I'm here. I could smell the gingerbread from the parlor." Louise leaned over the hot cookie sheet and inhaled slowly. "*Mmm.* It smells like Christmas in here. I take it the gingerbread is for your village. How did you get the cookies to look like boards?"

"I painted them before I baked them."

"Are you making a log cabin gingerbread house?"

"I'm making something different this year. I am using gingerbread for part of it, but I'm using sugar cookies too."

Louise poured a cup of tea and carried it to the table.

"What are you making?" Alice asked.

"You'll see." Jane wanted to make sure her project worked before she revealed her idea.

Alice was looking into her cup. Jane passed the plate of cookies to her. She looked up and Jane saw little furrows in her brow that weren't usually there.

"Is something wrong?"

"No, at least I hope not. Florence made a suggestion at the meeting tonight that she organize a cookie drive. I told them you have already planned a drive, and the church shouldn't compete with you. You *are* planning to include people at church, aren't you?" Alice's gaze held a question.

"Of course, I'd love to have people at church involved. I just don't want to make it a church event. I don't want this to get too big, but anyone is welcome to help if she or he wants to. What did the others say?"

"Lloyd spoke up to support you. The rest agreed. Florence backed off, but she wasn't happy about it. Have you asked people to help yet?"

"Clarissa and Carlene have volunteered. Lloyd offered to help. I'm sure Vera and Sylvia will help."

"Good," Alice said, clearly relieved. "You're far enough along that Florence can't take over."

The last thing Jane wanted was to stir up some kind of rivalry. "I'll call her and ask for cookies. Maybe that will be enough for her. Thanks for the heads-up."

⁓

The next morning after breakfast, Jane tidied up the kitchen. Once again, Alice had gone to work early. Though she worked part time, she often filled in for nurses who wanted time off over the holidays. Alice felt that those with children needed to be at home, not at the hospital. Jane had just started the dishwasher when Louise came in wearing her coat.

"What are your plans for today?" Jane asked.

"I have to practice the music for the Christmas Eve service and for this Sunday, so I'm going to spend the rest of the morning at church."

"I wish I could listen in but I really need to work on some things here. I'll see you at lunch."

After Louise had gone, Jane set out her cookie decorating supplies. She had bowls of red, green, blue, yellow, vanilla and chocolate decorator icing.

The stable was made of gingerbread. She'd painted rough boards with a mixture of food coloring and egg yolks before she baked the cookies, and she was pleased with the matte finish. She dusted the stable with powdered baking cocoa for a rugged, aged appearance, and then she frosted the three side edges together and attached a partial roof to make it stand for the backdrop. For contrast and texture, she created green frosting vines up the sides and roof.

The figures had simple faces, painted on before the sugar cookies were baked. She frosted Mary and Joseph with cream-colored robes and added rope frosting belts. The shepherd's robes were yellow and green, and frosting dots made the sheep fluffy white. She smooth-frosted the camels and cows a light tan, and the Wise Men had purple and blue robes decorated with bits of broken jewel-toned hard candies.

Standing back, she studied her creations, then pondered what to use for a base. She decided on a mixture of textures, using chopped nuts, brown-dyed coconut and crumbled whole wheat pasta for dirt and straw on a frosted piece of cardboard.

Jane centered the base on a place mat on the antique Queen Anne buffet in the dining room and arranged the stable on it. She then placed the decorated figures in the scene. Finally, she carefully balanced the angel on top of the stable.

The light from the dining room chandelier bathed the nativity in a soft glow. Jane stood back, amazed. The vibrant colors of the characters against the drab background made the scene more alive than she'd expected. Even built of cookies, the nativity touched a special place in her heart.

⌒

"I couldn't wait until Sunday," Patsy Ley said over the phone. Jane cradled the phone to her ear and sat down at the kitchen table. "I heard about the cookie drive, and I want to help. I hope I'm not being presumptuous."

"Not at all, Patsy. I'd love to have you be part of it. All you need to bring is two dozen of one kind of holiday cookie. Can Henry come with you? We're going out in teams to deliver the cookies."

"Oh yes, I know he'd love to do that. Do you need to know what kind of cookies I'm bringing?"

"No. I'm sure we'll get a good variety. Just bring a favorite."

"I'm so excited about this, Jane. We always had a cookie exchange when I was growing up. It's such fun. And even better that some of our homebound folks will get the fruits of our labors."

As Jane hung up, she opened her notebook to the page on the cookie drive. She added Patsy and Henry's names to the confirmed donor list. She needed to call the rest of her list. She punched in Sylvia Songer's number. She couldn't have a party without inviting her best friend. She got Sylvia's voice mail and left a call-back message; then she dialed the next number.

"Vera, this is Jane."

"Oh hi, Jane. Fred and Alice both mentioned your cookie drive. I hope your call means we're invited."

Jane laughed. "I wouldn't have a party without you and Fred. Can you come?"

"You bet. Do you need a lot of cookies? I can make a double batch."

"I think two dozen is enough, but I'll let you know if we need more."

"I'll bring four dozen anyway. There's no such thing as too many cookies. I'm thinking cherry thumbprint cookies. They're so easy, and good too."

Jane laughed. "I know they're good. I remember you made them last year for the Christmas Eve service. But I hear you on the easy part. I imagine you're superbusy right now."

"Things will slow down when school gets out for the holidays. The school Christmas program is tomorrow night if you can make it. The kids have really worked hard on it."

"Which means their teacher has worked doubly hard on it. Louise plans to go. Several of her piano students are involved. We'll see you there."

Jane left a message on Viola Reed's answering machine and decided she would stop in at Nine Lives Bookstore to see her in the morning. She should call Florence, but she wasn't in the mood to chat, so she'd put that off until tomorrow. So far she had six confirmed coming and bringing cookies, and she only had four people on her recipient list. She knew there must be more people who were homebound in the winter. She would ask around. After all, that was the purpose of the cookie drive—to make sure everyone felt loved and included at Christmastime.

❧

"When did you put up the cookie crèche scene, Jane?" Louise called from the dining room the next morning. "It's beautiful!"

Jane came from the kitchen followed by Alice. Inside the dining room, Alice stopped and stared. "Oh Jane, it's wonderful. I've never seen gingerbread look so, so *not* like gingerbread." She laughed.

"I put it together yesterday afternoon."

"And you didn't drag us in here to see it?" Alice asked.

Jane smiled. "I knew you'd see it soon enough."

❧

"Yoo-hoo." Aunt Ethel came in the back door. She stepped into the kitchen, wrapped in her heavy winter coat, a long purple woolen scarf and rabbit-fur earmuffs. Her rosy cheeks almost matched her Titian Dreams hair. "I hope you're finished with breakfast. I have news." She peeled off her coat and hat and hung them up, then pulled a notepad out of her purse.

"I've been working on our cookie drive," she announced, taking a seat at the kitchen table.

Jane was certain Ethel did not hear Jane's involuntary groan. Jane shot off a quick prayer that her aunt's enthusiasm and impulsiveness wouldn't turn her simple idea into a fiasco. "Would you like a cup of coffee and some breakfast?" Jane asked.

Ethel looked up. "That would be lovely. I've been so busy, I didn't have a proper breakfast."

"Help yourself," Alice said, indicating a plate of homemade sausage patties and bacon on the counter. "There's part of a cherry clafouti in the oven keeping warm."

"Thank you. I believe I will." She rose and put some of everything on a plate Jane handed to her.

Jane carried the butter dish, a small pitcher of maple syrup and silverware to the table.

"Thank you, dear. Now finish up so we can get down to business."

Wendell sauntered over and sat looking at Ethel's lap. He loved cuddling and loved leftover scraps even more. When Ethel spread a napkin in her lap and leaned forward, the cat stood, flipped his tail and returned to a corner where he could watch for any food that hit the floor.

Jane smiled at the cat's antics, then tilted her head toward the table, giving Louise and Alice a sign to leave the dishes until later and join Aunt Ethel. Alice fixed a cup of tea and Jane poured herself a cup of coffee. Louise declined but sat next to Ethel.

"All right," Ethel said, swallowing a bit of sausage. "I have good news. I've been talking to people downtown and at the churches and I've compiled a list of shut-ins. I took the liberty of extending our delivery area outside Acorn Hill. After all, those people in the country need cheering up too."

Jane breathed a sigh of relief. This time Aunt Ethel had really helped. She hadn't had time to compile a list, and she knew her aunt would be thorough. "Thank you, Auntie. That was very thoughtful of you."

"I want to do my part," Ethel said. "Here's the list." She handed Jane a piece of paper filled with names and addresses. It had thirty-four entries.

"Not all are elderly. Several people are at home recovering from accidents or surgery or illness."

Jane stared, aghast. If each team delivered to three homes, she'd need more than eleven teams. She had nowhere near that many people committed to bringing cookies and helping with deliveries. So far, she had fourteen dozen promised. She would make extras, of course, and she was sure Sylvia, Patsy and Clarissa would be happy to bring more.

"I still haven't decided what I'm making. I wish peaches were in season. Everyone likes my peach tarts so much, I could make miniatures." Ethel sighed. "Oh, and you know Duke Gladstone? He specifically requested *real* Christmas cookies."

"What kind is that?" Jane asked.

"I asked him the same thing. He gave me a look, as if I should know, then explained they are frosted, cut-out sugar cookies. He insisted any other types are fakes. Can you believe that?"

Jane laughed. "I guess we all have our favorites. And those are pretty traditional. I plan to make some *real* Christmas cookies, so I'll make sure he gets those."

That afternoon Jane could hear the drone of the vacuum cleaner coming from the parlor as she polished the mahogany dining room table. Alice was upstairs gathering laundry.

Jane poked her head in the parlor as Louise turned off the vacuum. "I'm done here, so I'm going to run downtown to do some errands. Do you need anything while I'm out?"

"Are you going by Nine Lives?" Louise asked. "The books I ordered for Cynthia's Christmas gift are in."

"I am. I want to see Viola about the cookie drive. I left her a message, but she's probably been too busy to call back."

"Good. Let me get a check. By the way, I want you to know I intend to make a batch of lemon cookies and a batch of Christmas Trixies for the cookie drive, so you can add those to your list."

"That's really sweet. Thanks." Louise wasn't a great cook. She and Alice left most of the cooking to Jane. But it boosted her spirits to know she had her sister's support. Just maybe they'd come up with enough cookies after all.

"Florence called me to discuss the choir," Louise said. "She wants the choir to be a team and go caroling as they deliver their cookies."

"The entire choir? Could they split up into teams of two?"

Louise shook her head. "I suggested that, but then there wouldn't be enough to harmonize. I know this isn't what you had in mind, but I think it'll be all right. I doubt all of them will participate. She said she would instruct everyone to bring cookies. "

Jane closed her eyes for a second. One way or another, Florence was determined to have her own part in the cookie drive. "All right. I'll put the choir down as a team."

"It'll work out."

"Yeah." Jane gave her sister a weak smile.

Louise went upstairs as Alice was coming down with an armload of laundry.

"Need anything in town?" Jane asked.

"I have an order at Time for Tea, if you wouldn't mind picking it up," Alice said.

"Happy to. I need to stop by for a few things there anyway."

"Is there anything I can do to help you get ready for the cookie swap or for Christmas?"

"That's really sweet, Alice. I plan to make several different kinds of cookies. You could roll dough and keep the pans washed."

Alice looked relieved. "Great. I'm good at doing dishes and I can follow directions. And I only work three days next week."

"I know I get carried away sometimes, so it means a lot that you and Louie want to do this with me."

"I love sharing Christmas with you and Louise," Alice said. "You liven things up just like Mother did."

Jane blinked back a tear. She'd never known Christmas with their mother, who had died when she was born. But to be compared to her was the ultimate compliment.

∽

A beautiful carol greeted Jane as she pushed open the door to Time for Tea. She enjoyed the classical music Wilhelm played in his store, but she rarely knew the name or composer. Louise always knew. This time, though, she had an answer.

"Good morning, Jane," Wilhelm greeted her.

"'Bring a Torch, Jeannette, Isabella,'" Jane announced, grinning.

Wilhelm laughed. "'*Un flambeau, Jeannette, Isabelle.*' A French carol from 1553. Very good."

She laughed. "I may not know classical music, but I know my Christmas carols. It's nice to see you in town for the holidays."

"I don't want Mother to be alone for Christmas.

However, I do have a trip planned to visit China after the new year. They produce a rare white tea there called Snow Buds, which is grown at a high elevation, and the tea is processed by hand in very small quantities. Very rare and delicate, with a complex taste. I hope to bring some back."

"Really? That sounds exotic. If you bring Snow Buds back, I'd like to buy some for Alice's birthday."

"I'll set some aside for you. I know she'll like it. So would you. What can I get for you today?"

"Alice asked me to pick up her order."

"Oh yes. I have it here." He produced a small bag. "Anything else?"

"I'd like a pound of your Christmas blend. And last year you had the large cinnamon sticks and cardamom pods and whole star anise. Do you have them this year?"

"In the jars on the wall. The bags are underneath. Making your own mulling spice?"

"Yes, and I use them for decorating, too, so I'll need quite a bit." Jane took a bag and filled it with long sticks of cinnamon bark. "How *is* your mother?" she asked as she filled another bag with cardamom pods.

"She's doing well, but it's hard for her to get

around these days. Especially when it's so cold. By the way, she heard about your cookie drive. She told me to ask if she can contribute some cookies. She's an excellent cook, you know."

"She wants to help? And I was going to ask if we should bring her a goody plate."

"You know she'd love a visit, but she isn't your typical shut-in. Friends stop by, and we have a caregiver who comes in twice a week. Mother wants to make *vanillekipferl*. It's a traditional German cookie. I used to help her make them when I was a boy. I told her I'd help her this year."

Jane was familiar with the little vanilla cookies. She tried to picture Wilhelm forming bits of dough into crescents. A labor of love for his mother. "I'd love to add her cookies to the trays. Do you think you and your mother could come to our cookie party on the twenty-second?"

"I'd be delighted to come, but Mother doesn't get out much, especially at night. She'll be content to contribute."

"Please thank her." Jane made a mental note to take part of the party to Wilhelm's mother that night.

After she left Time for Tea, Jane hurried down the block to the bookstore. The frigid air stung her cheeks and her breath puffed out in crystalline clouds. A tiny white flake drifted down and landed on her nose. Invigorated, she looked up. Sparkly crystals drifted around on the breeze, but there was too much steel-gray sky showing for snow. She made a little wish for snow as she pulled her scarlet knit scarf higher around her neck.

Strings of colored lights and silver tinsel garlands outlined the windows of Nine Lives Bookstore. Books, puzzles and parlor games were displayed amid gaily wrapped presents. In the middle of the display, Viola's tabby cat Diver was stretched out, showing his white belly, totally oblivious to the world. Jane opened the door and bells tinkled. Diver didn't twitch an ear, but Anna, the ivory Siamese, came up to rub against Jane's leg. Jane reached down and scratched her head. She looked up with her startling blue eyes and purred a warm welcome.

"Jane, good morning." Viola came out from behind a shelf of books wearing a gray wool skirt and red sweater, with a long Stewart plaid scarf around her neck. "I meant to return your phone call. Just haven't gotten to it yet. I'd love to bake cookies for your cookie drive. Such a nice idea."

"Great! You look Christmassy. Love your scarf."

"I bought it in Canada. Perfect for the season and the cold weather."

"You need it today for sure. Will you be able to come to the cookie party?"

"Oh yes. May I bring my new neighbors, Miriam and Sol Arens? I mentioned the drive to Miriam, and she thought it sounded like a wonderful idea."

"Of course. That'll be a good way for them to meet people."

"Oh yes. They are Jewish, so they're celebrating Hanukkah, but she told me she just loves the Christmas holidays. She wants to bring cookies."

"That's great. We'll be happy to have them part of the event."

"I knew you'd feel that way. Do you want to pick up Louise's books while you're here?"

"Yes. I told her I would."

"I'll get them."

Jane stopped at Wild Things on her way home. Stepping inside the floral shop was like being transported to a tropical paradise. The warm, moist scent of peat moss and the heady sweetness of flowers enveloped her, wiping away the cold outside.

"Jane, it's good to see you," Craig Tracy said, coming out from the back room.

"I should come in here every day, just to get a breath of spring."

Craig chuckled. "It looks like Christmas in here, in case you didn't notice."

"It's mostly red and white and green, but it smells like fresh dirt and, well, springtime."

"I heard you're having a cookie drive."

"It seems as if everyone in town has heard about it."

"Hey, this is Acorn Hill. You can't keep a secret here."

"Evidently not. Would you like to join us?"

"Do I have to make cookies?"

"No. But you could help us deliver them."

"In that case, I'd love to. Do you have Christmas plates for delivering the cookies?"

"Not yet."

"I get decorative aluminum ones for fruit arrangements. Let me supply them. I can donate the cellophane wrap and ribbon too. How many do you need?"

"A bunch. Aunt Ethel compiled a list of thirty-four."

"Really? I didn't realize we have that many who are homebound. I'll bring forty. If you need more, let me know."

"Wonderful! Thanks, Craig. I want to order an arrangement for the dining room table for the party. Something different. Not red."

"I have just the thing. I'll deliver it with the plates before the party."

⁓

That night Jane, Louise and Alice found seats near the back of the crowded elementary school auditorium. Jane waved at Vera, who was herding a group of angels to the front of the room.

"Is this seat taken?"

Jane turned to see Nia Komonos standing at the end of the row. "No. Come sit by me," Jane said, patting the metal folding chair.

Nia removed her coat, hat and knit gloves, then sat down. She was dressed in one of her signature tailored suits. A beaded red and green Christmas wreath pin adorned her collar, giving her a festive look.

"How have you been?" Jane asked.

"Oh, busy. Lots of the students have been to the

library trying to get in school projects before the Christmas break."

"I've been meaning to stop by the library. I don't know where time goes.'

Nia chuckled. "Same here. Can I elicit an invitation to your cookie party? Vera told me about it."

"You're on my list. I'm sorry I didn't call you yet. I'm kind of throwing this together at the last minute."

"With your talents, it will be a success. How many cookies do you need? I can make *Kourambiedes*. They're a Greek Christmas cookie that my mother used to make."

"If you could donate two dozen that would be wonderful."

Jane felt a tap on her shoulder and turned around. A young woman handed her a folded piece of paper.

"This came from someone in the back," she said.

Jane looked back at the several rows behind them. Dee Butorac, the high school history teacher, waved at her. When Jane held up the note, she nodded. Jane opened it. It had a name and address on it and a note. Stanley Shipman was convalescing at home from hip replacement surgery. Jane looked back at Dee and nodded. One more to add to the list to visit. Jane scribbled a note and sent it back to Dee, inviting her to join the party. She hadn't thought about Dee. But then she hadn't expected her idea to grow so big. Just a few close friends. She chuckled, drawing a look from Louise, who raised one eyebrow. Just then the lights dimmed and the curtains parted. Jane shrugged and turned her attention to the stage.

$\backsim$

"I'm glad you came by the shop yesterday. I kept thinking about calling you, then I'd get busy." Sylvia Songer stood in the inn's kitchen the next evening, looking at the array of greens and berries Jane had spread out on the newspaper-covered table. Jane had wanted to make outdoor luminaries, and had invited her friend to make some too.

"I knew you were running craft classes all day, so I didn't want to call and interrupt you. I figured I'd catch you when you had a break."

"The classes have been packed. Seems like everyone is making gifts this year. Can you believe it's only seven days till Christmas?"

"No. Time is just flying. I'm trying to make gifts

for Louise and Alice, but I never seem to find time to work on them when they're gone and we're not busy."

"Well, I'm excited about this craft," Sylvia said, turning her focus to the table. "I'm also intrigued. I love luminaries, but I've always made them out of paper bags."

"I see you brought plastic jugs," Jane said.

"I did." She lifted a large bulging black plastic bag.

"I'll get mine and we'll start. If you have jugs with handles, use the heavy scissors and cut around them just below the handle."

Jane retrieved empty plastic gallon milk containers and wide mouth pint canning jars from the pantry.

When the jugs were cut down to bowl size, Jane packed the bottom of each with a layer of mountain laurel leaves and small evergreen sprigs that she'd cut for decorating. "This gives a bit of cushion and space for the ice to form. Then I start up the sides with flowers and leaves and pine sprigs or anything I want to put in, like so."

They used poinsettia blooms, evergreen sprigs and holly berries, lining the plastic jugs. "Don't make it too dense. You want the light to shine through the luminaries."

"So when we're done, the ice is like a floral sculpture?"

"Right. Now we'll insert the jar in the middle to hold everything in place." Jane set the pint jar inside the plastic tub of greens and flowers, carefully rearranging so it sat in the center. Jane secured the luminaries with strips of tape.

"I love these. Too bad it takes a cold snap to be able to use them. They'd melt pretty fast if the temperature gets above freezing," Sylvia said.

"I made wax luminaries in San Francisco. Same idea, only I'd fill heavy-gauge helium balloons with warm water and use them to mold wax instead of using jars. I'd coat the insides of the milk jugs with hot wax and then embed my greens and flowers, then add wax to the bottom and set my water balloon inside and keep adding melted wax until it filled up the sides."

They made more. Eight for Sylvia, who would use them outside her store, and sixteen for Jane, who wanted to line the front and side walkways. They carried the jugs out to the back porch, then took bottles of distilled water and carefully filled the gaps between the jugs and the glass jars. The jars wanted to float, but the tape held them down. Standing back, they surveyed their handiwork. The jugs filled the porch and part of the sidewalk. "Now we wait until they freeze."

"I'll help you clean up our mess," Sylvia said.

"Do you have time for a cup of tea and some cookies?"

"Does Santa wear a red suit and go 'Ho, ho, ho'?"

It was midafternoon when Jane finally sat down with a cup of coffee and her list. December 19 and she still didn't have enough cookies for all the shut-ins. She would have to bake enough to fill out all the plates.

She got out her recipes. She had to make her version of mocha krinkles. They were a favorite. And she would make the Christmas icebox cookies and ginger crackles and perhaps the self-frosting fennel drops from her mother's cookbook. She needed to make a double batch of her mother's butter horns for Christmas morning and also to serve at the party.

As she flipped through her recipes, she came across one for marshmallows. She hadn't made marshmallows in years. They would be good for the cookie party. She could coat some in chocolate for the goody plates and serve some with hot chocolate. On a cold night, that might be a big hit.

Marshmallows were a lot simpler to make than most people realized, and they tasted divine. Especially with a swirl of caramel, or coffee and cocoa powder, or a few crunches of crushed candy cane. She decided that they were the first things she'd tackle.

She was just pouring the gooey marshmallow mixture into a greased pan to set when Alice came in toting sacks of groceries. She set two bags on the counter.

"Need any help?" Jane asked.

"No. I'll get them. I'm already bundled up. Your ice bowls look like they're set. I hear it got down to twelve degrees last night."

"Really? I knew it was cold. I'll leave them out there until Sylvia comes over tonight, and we'll unmold them. I've just finished making marshmallows and am about to start some cookies."

"Let me clean up the bowls while you put the groceries away. Then you'll know where everything is," Alice said. "I'll start as soon as I bring in the rest of the groceries and then I can keep up as you continue to bake."

"Thanks, Alice, but you don't have to. You've already run errands for me."

"I promised to help. Besides, I want to. My hands are freezing. The hot water will feel heavenly."

࿂

Sylvia came by soon after the Howard sisters finished their dinner.

"I can't wait to set these up and light the candles," she said as she and Jane carried two luminaries into the kitchen. "I'll help you unmold yours. I'll take mine in the tubs and unmold them at home, so they don't melt in my car."

"You can put that in the sink," Jane said. She'd filled it with hot tap water. "It won't take too long."

As the ice started to melt, the sculpture came loose. Jane removed the tape and pulled it out by the glass jar insert. She carried it out the front door and set it on the side of the walk. When she got back inside, Sylvia had unmolded the second one and gone out the back to bring in two more.

"This is sure easier with two people," Jane said. She carried luminaries out as Sylvia freed them from the jugs. When she had four pairs lining each side of the front walk, they took votive candles, soft wax to hold them in place and a fire starter, and secured a candle in each luminary.

Jane lit them off, and then they stood back and surveyed their handiwork. The luminaries showed a soft glow of candlelight that grew stronger as they warmed up. "They get better," Jane said.

"I think they're lovely," Sylvia said. "With the lights trimming the house and the porch, the inn will look like a Christmas fairy tale."

"A cold fairy tale. Let's get inside. I'm offering hot chocolate with homemade marshmallows."

"That sounds yummy, but I'll have to take a rain check. I want to get my luminaries home and set up tonight, and we still have yours for the back walk."

"You go on. I'll take care of them. Thanks for your help. I'll give you a hand loading them into your trunk."

As Jane walked back from Sylvia's car the luminaries glowed cheerily along the walkway. She'd bought fifteen-hour votive candles and hoped to get two nights out of each candle until Christmas Eve. Then she would let them burn all night to symbolize waiting and watching for the birth of the Christ child.

The fennel drops had to cure before she baked them, so Jane mixed the ingredients right after breakfast, then put teaspoonfuls of the drop cookie dough on pans, swirled them into circles and set them aside. She would bake them the next morning.

Cheese balls were on her list of appetizers, and they needed time for the flavors to meld, so she got out her cheeses. She mixed a batch of grated Swiss and cream cheese with a dash of nutmeg, pepper and mayonnaise. She added diced maraschino cherries, formed a ball, then rolled it in sliced almonds. She made another ball of blended aged cheddar and cream cheese with a bit of mustard and Worcestershire sauce and fresh chopped parsley. She mixed in sliced pimento olives, formed a ball, then rolled it in chopped pecans. She wrapped the balls in plastic wrap and stored them in the refrigerator.

"Do you need anything from Potterston?" Alice asked her as she washed the bowls and beaters for Jane. "I'm working half a shift this afternoon, so I could stop at the store on my way home."

"Thanks, but I need to do a bit of shopping myself."

Louise was at the table, addressing Christmas cards. "Would you mind dropping these in the mail for me?"

"Happy to."

"When are you going to town, Jane? Perhaps I could make cookies while you're gone," Louise said.

"You're really going to make cookies?" Alice asked.

"Of course," Louise said.

"Not me. I'll do anything else but that."

Jane grinned, "Louie, you don't have to bake. I can make enough to represent all of us."

"O ye of little faith," Louise said, placing her hand over her heart. "I can do this and you'll like them."

"Or else?" Alice said with a laugh.

"*Hmph.*" Louise raised her eyebrows in a mock glare.

"Okay. You can have the kitchen as soon as we're done cleaning up," Jane said.

"Good. I bought all my ingredients. I'll get started right away."

⌒

Jane loved browsing in Acorn Hill Antiques. Though she wasn't an antique buff like Louise, she appreciated the artistry of the past. Soft lighting, muted colors and a faint musty scent like lavender and old paper hit Jane's senses. Pleasant. Comfortable. She smiled at Rachel Holzmann, who looked up from behind the counter where she was sorting invoices.

"Good morning, Jane. Merry Christmas. May I help you with something?"

"Merry Christmas to you too. I thought I'd look around. I'm making presents for Louise and Alice, and I need small frames or some decorative way to display small pictures."

"We have some frames on the back wall," she said, pointing.

"Thanks. I'll look." Jane wandered to the rear of the store. Most of the frames were too large, but back in the far corner on a shelf was an old-fashioned hinged double frame with pictures of an elderly lady and gentleman. The frame was metal, with a copper, brass and bronze floral pattern. Jane picked it up. The size was right. If she split it in half, she'd have two matching frames. It was in very good shape. The price was reasonable. She carried it to the counter.

"This is exactly what I need," Jane said, getting out her wallet.

"I'm glad. Let me wrap it in tissue." Rachel took

the price sticker off and wrapped it carefully and put it in a small paper sack. She rang up the sale. "We drove by the inn last night and saw your luminaries. They are beautiful," she said as she handed Jane the bag.

"Thanks. I heard you're leaving before Christmas."

"We take off tomorrow night. That's why I'm scrambling to get everything in order. We'll visit friends in New York, then drive south on a buying trip. We'll be gone all of January. We're closing the store while we're gone. January is usually pretty slow."

"I'm sorry you won't be here for our cookie drive. I think it's going to be a lot of fun."

"I know, and I'm sorry to miss it. If we'd known… But we'd already made plans."

"Of course. I hope you have a wonderful trip." Jane smiled.

"Oh we will. But Joseph and I want to help with the cookie drive, even though we can't be there. Here is our contribution," she said, handing Jane an envelope. "I was going to bring it by the inn after work."

Jane looked at the envelope. She could tell it had money in it. What was she to do with it? "That's very nice, Rachel, but we're just doing simple cookie plates. We really don't need—"

"Please, Jane, we want to help. I know you'll find a way to use it. And if you don't, you can give it to the church."

"All right. Thank you, Rachel. Have a great holiday."

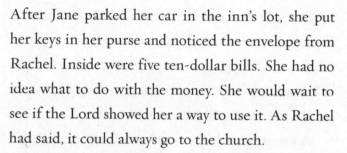

After Jane parked her car in the inn's lot, she put her keys in her purse and noticed the envelope from Rachel. Inside were five ten-dollar bills. She had no idea what to do with the money. She would wait to see if the Lord showed her a way to use it. As Rachel had said, it could always go to the church.

When Jane opened the kitchen door, she found Louise still working in the kitchen, and the smells were wonderful. Jane removed her coat and gloves by the back door.

"Need any help?" she asked.

"No thank you. I have everything under control."

A tray of small yellow cookies was cooling on the counter.

"May I try one?" Jane asked.

"They aren't finished until I frost them, but yes, you may."

Louise stopped and watched as Jane popped one in her mouth.

"*Mmm*. That's really good. Very lemony."

Louise beamed.

Jane was tempted to hang around and see what else Louise was baking, but she needed the time to work on her gifts. She went up to her room and put a CD of contemporary Christmas songs in her portable player, then got out the quilling she'd started. Absentmindedly humming along to the music, she began rolling quill pieces to make a filigree mat for each of the photographs.

A knock on her door made her jump. She'd been concentrating so hard, she hadn't even realized the music had stopped. She covered her work with a scarf and went to the door, barely opening it, so her sister couldn't see past her.

Alice looked at her quizzically. "It's time to go to the Coffee Shop for dinner."

Jane glanced at her watch. Nearly six. "Can I have five minutes?"

"Certainly. Meet us downstairs."

They sat at the last available table at the Coffee Shop. Hope Collins looked over and gave them a little wave as she took an order from another table.

"I talked to Rose Bellwood today," Alice said. "Tonight is the last night of their living nativity at the farm, so she and Samuel can attend the party. She's bringing cookies from her daughter-in-law too."

"Great! I'm glad they can come. And bless Rose," Jane said. "I've been concerned that we won't have enough cookies. That will really help."

"What can we do to help get ready before tomorrow night?" Louise asked. "I finished my cookies today, so I plan to dust and run the vacuum tomorrow. What else do you need?"

"I'm available too," Alice said.

"I just need to make finger foods for the party. When everyone arrives, they can have hors d'oeuvres while we arrange the cookies on plates and wrap them. Then we divide up into teams to deliver them. I'm not sure how we will do that. I thought married couples could go as teams and we can match up the others."

"The carolers will be one big team," Louise said. "But they won't stay long at any house, so they can take several plates."

"True." Jane hoped the teams would visit with the homebound, rather than hand them a plate of cookies and leave, but the choir would give pleasure with their music, so she supposed that was sufficient.

Hope came over to take their orders. "I'm so excited about your cookie swap! I've got the day off, so I'm making cookies and so is my friend Betsy. We want to be a team for delivering the goodies, you know. Is that all right?"

"Yes, that's great! I'll put you down." She opened her purse and removed a small notepad. Hope held up her order pad. "And I'd better get your order, before we run out of food. The special is roast beef, mashed potatoes and gravy. And there's apple raspberry pie for dessert. If you want pie, you'd better order it now so I can set it aside."

They ordered three specials and three slices of pie à la mode. Hope left to turn in their order.

"Sounds like you're getting a great response for the cookie drive," Louise said. "Are you going to have enough now?"

"With cookies from Rose, Hope, Betsy and you, Louise, we've got to be close."

"Have you called the homebound folks to let them know we're coming?" Alice asked.

"Oh no!" Jane stared at her sisters. "I can't believe I didn't think of that. I'll have to make calls in the morning. I wonder what else I've forgotten."

"Don't worry about it. I can make calls tomorrow. You've done all the planning so far, and it's turned into much more than any of us expected," Alice said.

"I'll help too," Louise said.

Jane let out a deep sigh. She smiled at her sisters. "What would I do without you two?"

Louise laughed. "We've wondered that for years."

Jane sat in the living room, her Bible and a notebook in her lap, sipping from a cup of cocoa with a puffy, melting homemade marshmallow floating on top. She finished her morning devotions and said a special prayer that the cookie drive would bless those who gave and those who received.

The colored lights on the Christmas tree sparkled and illuminated the delicate glass ornaments. It was still dark outside the windows. She'd lighted the candles on the mantel, and they cast a cheerful glow on the room and all the decorations and green-ery. Jane loved Christmas. She loved all the holidays, but Christmas was the best. She remembered sitting with Louise and Alice listening to their father read the Christmas account in the book of Luke. His deep voice grew reverent as he told the story. That was one of Jane's favorite memories. She loved the fun of the holidays. From the decorations to the food to the joy that seemed to abound, Christmas was whimsi-cal and charming and heartwarming. But best of all, she loved celebrating the most important event in all of history. The event that brought hope to the world. Thinking about that as she sipped the rich dark chocolate, she hoped the cookie party that night would spread a reminder of that hope to her friends and the homes they would visit.

After a quick breakfast of hot cereal, Jane went over her list again. Alice and Louise were cleaning, leav-ing her free to cook. She'd already prepared some of the ingredients she'd need.

She still wasn't sure how many were coming. How would she divide them into teams? Draw numbers?

Jane liked things organized, like a recipe. This party was not organized to her satisfaction.

After a few minutes, she gave up and put her pen down. She looked up at the ceiling, but her gaze was fixed far beyond. "Okay, Lord, this is in Your hands. I have no idea how it's going to work out."

⁓

The house was ready. The calls were made. The hors d'oeuvres were well in hand. Louise had covered the dining room table with a fine white linen cloth. Craig's stunning floral arrangement of snowball chrysanthemums, carnations and lilies, with waxy green leaves, silver candles, eucalyptus and blue spruce and tall silver sprayed twigs on a silver charger graced the center of the dining room table. Samovars for the hot spiced cider and hot chocolate looked elegant on a side table.

Aunt Ethel and Lloyd arrived first, followed by Florence and Ronald Simpson. Alice took their plates of cookies and put them in the kitchen. Then Rev. Thompson came in with a tray of brownies.

"These look yummy, Pastor Ken," Alice said. "Did you make them?"

"I did," he said, looking pleased at the compliment. "With the help of a boxed mix." He smiled.

"Mixes are wonderful, aren't they?" Louise said. "I used one for my cookies too."

"You did?" Jane said. "And here I thought you made them from scratch."

"I never claimed that."

Jane laughed. "No you didn't, and they're delicious. I didn't expect you to bring goodies, Ken. It's enough that you're taking time to join us."

"I wouldn't have missed it." He glanced around. "From the look of all the cars outside, everyone in town feels the same way."

"Let me take your coat so you can warm up with some hot cider or cocoa," Alice said.

"Thanks, Alice."

Jane and Louise went to carry trays of food to the dining room. Cheese platters, miniature meatballs on skewers with pineapple chunks and a fruit platter. Marinated shrimp. Miniature red and green cheese-filled pepper poppers. Assorted crackers with the cheese balls. Marinated, pickled mushrooms. Deviled eggs.

The front door never stayed shut for long. A steady stream of party guests with platters of cookies kept arriving. Jane had made miniature puffs filled with chicken salad, and others stuffed with cherries and custard.

"Wow, I've never seen so many cookies in one place," Sylvia said, carrying her frosted sugar cookies into the kitchen. Every counter and the table were covered with trays of cookies.

"This isn't all of them. And it looks like we've got about two dozen people out there already."

Jane stood in the middle of the kitchen and looked around. "Good thing we have a lot of homes to cover. Want to help me split up the cookies?"

"Sure. Have you eaten?"

"No. I've been too busy."

"Let me bring us each a plate of food to nibble on. Your food looks fabulous."

Louise looked through the doorway. "Come say hi to everyone, Jane. This is your party, after all. Don't worry about the cookies. We'll get to them."

Jane pushed her hair behind her ear. "You're right." She took off her apron. When she stepped out of the kitchen, someone exclaimed, "Jane!"

The guests began clapping. As she greeted her friends, she was surrounded by hugs and affectionate greetings.

"Jane, these are my neighbors, Miriam and Sol," Viola said.

"I'm so glad you could come." Jane extended a welcome hand to her guests. "Have you met everyone?"

"Yes, Viola introduced us. This is such a lovely idea. Thank you for letting us join your celebration," Sol said.

Miriam gave Jane a container of bright blue and white frosted cookies. "Viola suggested we bring something that is traditional at our house. These are *dreidel* cookies. A dreidel is a traditional toy top that children play a game with during Hanukkah."

"These look wonderful. Thank you."

Clara Horn came in with Hope Collins and Betsy Long. She spotted Jane and made her way through the crowded hallway.

"I brought dog and kitty cookies," she said, handing Jane a plastic bag filled with individually wrapped cookies shaped like bones and mice. "I made them myself. It's Daisy's favorite cookie."

"How thoughtful. Where is Daisy tonight?" Clara seldom went anywhere without her miniature Vietnamese potbellied pig.

"She's at home. Daisy doesn't like crowds, you know. She's afraid of getting stepped on."

"Of course. You can put your coat in the parlor and help yourself to some hors d'oeuvres."

"Thank you. I will."

Hope Collins smiled as Clara walked off. "She sure spoils that pig. Pet cookies is a pretty good idea, though. I bet no one else brought any."

"You're right. Those look delicious," Jane said, taking the container of cookies from Hope.

"Oatmeal with macadamia nuts, white chocolate, dark chocolate and cherries," Hope said.

"I made plain chocolate chip," Betsy said. "I hope that's all right."

"Chocolate chips are always in season, and these look wonderful."

"Do you need any help in the kitchen?" Hope asked.

"Not tonight. This is your night off. Go enjoy yourself."

Hope grinned. "You don't have to tell me twice." She and Betsy made their way to the end of the table where the plates were.

"I think everyone is here who's coming," Alice said.

"Considering half the town is here, I'd agree," Louise said. "Are all the appetizers out?"

"There are more in the pantry," Jane said. "Every

inch of kitchen counter space is covered with cookies. I'd better start dividing them."

"I sent a team in to work on them already," Louise said. "Let me take those in. What's in the bag?"

"Doggie and kitty cookies," Jane said. "We have to make sure they don't get mixed in with the others."

Alice laughed. "I'll take charge of that. But do we know which of our deliveries have pets?"

"No clue. Perhaps we can send a couple with each team," Jane said. "Leave one for Wendell. Where is he, anyway?"

"Hiding from all the feet," Alice said. "Louise and I will get the guests split up into teams. How many do we need?"

"At least twelve teams of two or more. We have thirty-six homes to visit," Jane said.

"Other than the choir, we have enough people for two to three per team," Louise said.

"Great. I divided the deliveries by location. Make sure you put me on a team. And I'll go see how the cookie plates are coming." Jane left her sisters and went into the kitchen.

Sylvia and Vera had thirty-six plates set out on the table and counters, and containers of cookies were stacked everywhere. They were busy filling the plates with cookies.

"How's it coming?"

"I'd say your cookie drive is a success," Sylvia said. "I've never seen such a variety of cookies. We do have a lot of frosted sugar cookies, though. I didn't realize they're so popular."

"I think word got out about Duke and his fondness for sugar cookies," Vera said.

"I've also put some of what he considers *faux* Christmas cookies on his plate. They look so delicious, though, I doubt he'll be able to resist them."

There was a flurry of activity as teams got ready to leave. Louise went with the choir team. Alice left with Rev. Thompson and Wilhelm Wood, and Craig Tracy and Jane partnered.

"I'll drive" Craig said. "You must be exhausted after putting together this event. Highly successful, by the way."

"Thanks, Craig. Who is on our list?"

"Let's see. We've got Evelyn Potter, Hazel Tucker and Duke Gladstone."

Jane laughed. "I should have known Alice and Louise would give me Duke." She shrugged on her coat and slipped on her gloves. "Here are the cookie plates. I'm ready."

Craig took two of the red cellophane–wrapped plates and followed Jane out the front door. "Your luminaries are stunning," he said as they walked down the sidewalk. "I wonder if I could figure out a way to make permanent ones."

⌒

"Who is it?"

"It's Jane Howard and Craig Tracy, Miss Potter." Jane could hear Christmas music as two latches unlocked and the door creaked open. Jane smiled. "Merry Christmas, Miss Potter. We brought a plate of Christmas goodies for you."

"Well isn't that dandy? Come on in. Your sister called this morning to say someone would come by tonight. I'm glad it's you, Jane. I was just watching the Radio City Christmas show on television. I love the precision of the Rockettes and their choreography is wonderful."

"Miss Potter was my dance teacher when I was a

girl," Jane told Craig. As her former teacher preceded them into the living room, Jane noted that the elderly woman still moved with grace, even though she leaned on a cane.

"You may call me Evelyn. Would you like a glass of apple juice?" she asked them.

"No thank you, we just ate."

"All right then. Let me sit down. I can't stand for long." Her gnarled hands shook and she collapsed into the chair as if her legs wouldn't hold her up. "Come sit and visit an old lady for a while. I'm delighted to have company."

"That's why we're here," Craig said.

Jane handed her the cookie plate.

"Oh how lovely!" She hooked her cane on the arm of her Queen Anne chair. "I used this cane as a prop. Do you remember, Jane? You used it in a tap routine."

"I do remember. I loved my dancing lessons. And I always thought you were the best dancer in the world."

Evelyn chuckled. "I used to kick up a pretty good leg, but I was never as good as those girls," she said, pointing to the television. She'd turned off the volume, but the long line of dancing girls kicked as high as the tops of their heads in perfect unison.

Next to the television, rotating slowly, was a tall vintage aluminum Christmas tree. On the floor in front of it was a spinning color wheel, throwing red, green, orange and blue light onto the tree, causing it to sparkle and change colors as it turned. It was decorated with red and green balls.

"I haven't seen an aluminum tree in years," Craig said.

"Those trees were the height of fashion when I was a young woman," Evelyn said. "And I was pleased as punch that I could afford to splurge and buy that tree. It's lasted well, don't you think?"

"Very well," Jane said. A set of bisque kewpie-style carolers held center stage on an old walnut radio console. Vintage lights were strung around the windows. "I love your decorations."

"Thank you. I'm partial to them myself. They hold so many memories." Evelyn was untying the ribbon on the cookie plate. She pulled back the wrapping. "Oh, these look divine." Evelyn offered them a cookie.

"No thanks. We had some before we came. But please go ahead," Jane said, sitting down next to Craig on the couch.

Evelyn selected a linzer cookie and took a small

bite. "Mmm. Delicious. I was just thinking today about Christmas in Acorn Hill during the war. I was a telephone operator with Civil Defense, you know."

"I didn't know that," Jane said.

"Yes. We were set up in the basement of the courthouse in Potterston. We had air raid tests all the time. Our system came in real handy for emergencies. If someone needed help, the party line phone system helped to spread the word. Anyone could listen in on calls on their line. But our emergency system was more efficient to rally police and fire crews and medical help."

"Like the 911 system," Craig said. "Is that how it started?"

"No, that was years later. We were all wrapped up in the war back then. Lots of our local boys were overseas. Here at home, we all tried to do our part. I wanted to be a welder or a riveter, but the factories were in the big cities. My George needed me helping on the farm."

"Food was scarce, so I imagine farms were really important to keeping the country going," Jane said.

"Very true. I remember the food rationing. It was always tough, but we really felt it during the holidays.

We got ration coupons for our allotment of sugar, but it was so precious and scarce, it wasn't always available. And what is Christmas without cookies and fruitcake?"

"I've read some of the recipes from the war. You were very creative," Jane said.

"Indeed we were. George and I had some sugar maples at the farm. We'd tap the sap and make our own maple syrup. I substituted it for sugar in recipes. I made cookies and pudding and candy and sweet popcorn. My favorite treat was maple fudge. Oh my, it's better than pralines." She closed her eyes, remembering. "And the maple was wonderful on home-cured ham."

"Sounds like you managed pretty well," Jane said.

"Oh we did, because everyone in town shared. We raised hogs and chickens, so we had pork and eggs to share, and vegetables from our root cellar. Our neighbors raised turkeys, so we traded. We had turkey for Christmas dinner and they had one of our hams. We were fortunate, out here in the country. They weren't so lucky in the cities. And we never forgot that our troops overseas were suffering."

"War is terrible," Jane said.

"Yes, but we had some wonderful times. We had a lot of snow one year, so we hitched our mule to the old sleigh and drove to town for Christmas Eve services. We picked up two families on our way to Grace Chapel. We sang Christmas carols and forgot about the war for a little while. I don't mind being housebound most of the time. I keep busy, but I miss church. Watching preachers on television just isn't the same."

"Would you like to go to the Christmas Eve service this year?" Craig asked, surprising Jane. "I'd be happy to come and get you."

"Oh my. I don't know. I don't move very well, you know."

"You can move as slowly as you must. I'll pick you up early so there's plenty of time. If necessary, I'll carry you to the car and into the church. What do you say?"

Jane caught a look of desire and distress in Evelyn's gaze. She suddenly realized it took more to go out than getting from the house to a car. "I can come by early and help you get ready," she offered.

"Bless your heart, Jane Howard. And you, Craig Tracy. I say I'd like that very much. Thank you."

❦

"The door's open. Come in," a shaky voice called from inside the blue clapboard house.

Craig opened the door and Jane went in first. "Mrs. Tucker, it's Jane Howard and Craig Tracy."

"Come in the living room. I've been expecting you. I'm sorry I can't get up to greet you properly."

Hazel Tucker's white hair barely covered her head in fine wisps. She was sitting in a recliner, her feet raised and a soft blue lap blanket over her feet and legs. She had on a heavy sweater. She'd always seemed old to Jane. Now she seemed ancient.

A single lamp cast dim light on the room. A small, artificial Christmas tree sat in the corner, covered with lovely old glass ornaments, but no Christmas lights. The walls were decorated with Norman Rockwell prints of the four seasons and of the old-fashioned town and townspeople that he made famous.

"We brought you some Christmas goodies," Jane said.

Craig moved forward and handed the plate to the old lady. "Merry Christmas, Mrs. Tucker."

Her eyes lit up as she took the brightly wrapped

offering. "Bless your hearts. This is lovely. I do love sweets. I don't cook anymore, though. I get meals delivered every day. Please, pull up a chair and visit with me for a bit. I'm sorry I don't have something to offer you."

"We are just fine," Jane said. "Let me turn on another light. It's pretty dim in here."

"Don't bother. I can see well enough."

"All right. Can I fix you a cup of tea to have with a cookie?"

"No, no. Thank you, dear. If I drink tea this late, I'll have to get up during the night. I use a walker, but I don't navigate too well. I'll save the cookies to have with my pills right before bed. I have to eat something with my medicine, you know."

Craig got two straight-back chairs from the kitchen table and set them close to the recliner and they sat down. "I miss having you come into the flower shop," Craig said. "Hazel used to stop in for cut flowers. If I'd known we were coming to your house, I'd have brought some. I'll bring you some tomorrow," he promised.

"You don't have to do that," she said, but she looked so pleased Jane knew she would welcome his flowers and his attention.

"I remember you led the children's choir at

church, didn't you?" Jane turned to Craig. "Mrs. Tucker taught my Sunday school class and she taught English at the junior high school."

"Please call me Hazel. After all, you're an adult now. I remember when you were just a little tyke. You were a tomboy. You turned into a fine woman, though. Your mother and father would be proud of you."

"Thank you, Hazel." Jane smiled. "I hear I was quite a handful."

"You were rather energetic, but you weren't the only tomboy in the family. Your sister Alice had her moments."

"Alice? I didn't know that."

"Oh yes. Your first Christmas, Louise and Alice volunteered you for baby Jesus in the church's living nativity play. Louise insisted it didn't matter that you were a girl. You were a baby, so people wouldn't know the difference. Louise played Mary so that she could care for you and Alice was a shepherd. She was supposed to control the sheep. Your father was there keeping an eye on things."

"Was there more than one animal?" Craig asked.

"Oh my, yes. Alice had two sheep on ropes.

Lloyd Tynan was another shepherd, but he had a goat and a cow." Hazel laughed. "They didn't have a real camel, so they put some kind of hump on an old horse. He looked ridiculous. Something spooked the sheep and they took off down the hill toward town, bleating and making an awful ruckus. Alice chased after them. You should have seen her. Her robe and headdress were flying in the wind and she was yelling at the sheep. That made them run faster. Your father ran after her. She caught one, but the other one ran the other way. Your father rescued her and they managed to round up the escapee. That was the one and only time the church held a living nativity. Some years later, when Sam and Rose Bellwood started their family, they had the nativity at their farm."

"They still do," Jane said. "They held it for several nights."

"With their feed and stalls right there, at least the animals won't go anywhere."

"Hazel, would you like a ride to church on Christmas Eve? I'm picking up Evelyn Potter, and I'd be happy to take you too," Craig said.

"Oh dear, no. I can't take the cold. No matter

how much I put on, it cuts right though to my bones. But you've brought me joy tonight. Thank you so much for coming."

⌒

It was snowing softly when Craig and Jane stepped outside. Jane thrilled at the lovely white flurries. She hoped it would snow enough to cover the ground and give them a white Christmas.

"Did you notice how cold it was in Hazel's house?" Jane asked as they drove away.

"I did."

"I wonder if she keeps the house cold and the lights low to bring her utility bills down."

"I was thinking the same thing," Craig said.

Their last stop was Duke Gladstone. He shuffled along slowly, but he looked dapper in a bright red sweater vest. A railroad cap sat on top of his shock of white hair. He'd been expecting them and anticipating a plate of *real* Christmas cookies. He unwrapped the plate and smiled when he saw the frosted sugar cookies. He then peeked underneath the top layer of cookies.

"And what have we here? Fakes." He let out an

exaggerated sigh. "I don't know why people insist on making all these other things, when there's only one kind of real Christmas cookie. But I wouldn't want to hurt anyone's feelings. I'll suffer through them," he said, a twinkle in his eyes.

A retired railroad engineer, Duke showed Jane and Craig his model train room, all decorated for Christmas. There were two trains in front of an old-fashioned station.

"One of your trains is off the track," Craig said.

Toward the back of the table, a train lay on its side. Tiny people stood around it. A model of an old car and bus were parked by the train.

"Well you see, that's what really happened. That was a Christmas I'll never forget. I was working the line and a train derailed on icy tracks just outside of Acorn Hill. Fortunately, no one was hurt badly, but all those people were traveling to spend Christmas with family or friends. Soon as we got the word out, town folks showed up with cars and buses to bring the visitors to town. The churches and school opened up and ladies brought in blankets and pillows and food they were going to have for their own family Christmas. The stores and restaurants sent food to make sure no one went hungry." Duke shook his head, his gaze intent on his display.

"That must have been quite an event," Craig said.

"Sure was. Me and the missus took a family home with us, but I had to go back out and help clean up the mess. The man went with me. As we went out, we could hear singing and laughing. Turned out to be more an adventure than a tragedy, thanks to the people in this town. I never saw anything like it again, but this town knows how to celebrate Christmas in the real spirit, you know. I witnessed that firsthand. It took all night to get the tracks cleared and get another train to take the folks on their way. The couple that stayed with us sent us Christmas cards for years after that."

$\backsim$

"I'd have to agree with Duke," Craig said as they left. "Acorn Hill does have a full measure of the real spirit of Christmas. Thanks for letting me be part of it this year, Jane."

"It was fun, wasn't it? I hope everyone had as great a time as we did."

When Jane got home, Alice handed her an envelope. "This is from the ANGELs. They wanted to help someone who is elderly, so they cut and sold pine and fir boughs door to door. Carol Matthews gave it to me. I don't know what you want to do with it, but here it is."

"That's not the only one," Louise said. She reached into her pocket. "A visitor to the Bellwoods' nativity last night wanted to do something nice for someone and gave this to Samuel. Since you organized the cookie drive, he thought you might know how it could be used."

Jane stared at the envelope and the wad of bills from her sisters. She got out her purse and took out the envelope inside.

"I didn't plan this, and I was at a loss when Rachel Holzmann insisted I take this money, but tonight I found out what it's for. Hazel Tucker is living in an ice-cold house. She's wrapped up in blankets, sitting in a dark house, with only one bulb burning. She didn't even have lights on her Christmas tree. Craig and I got the impression she can't afford her utilities."

Jane had opened the envelopes and smoothed

out the bills. She'd counted them out. Three hundred and forty dollars. Suddenly she had a lump in her throat at the generosity of their friends and neighbors. She'd had an idea for a small, simple cookie swap. She hadn't counted on the hearts of the people of Acorn Hill. Jane had a feeling the gift of cash would miraculously stretch to keep Hazel warm through the long winter.

*T*hat cookie drive provided the best assortment of cookies that I've ever seen in one place," Alice said. "I even liked your cookies, Louise."

"Thank you...I think. I forget how you handled the donations, Jane."

"The next morning I took that money to the utility company. When they heard about Hazel's problem, they were happy to apply it to her account. They called her while I was there and told her that an anonymous gift had covered her heat for the winter. I stopped to see her before the Christmas Eve service, and her house was warm and there were lights on her Christmas tree. Craig had brought her a lovely bouquet. She glowed from more than the heat."

Jane fell silent for a moment, smiling at the memory. "But the best part of that Christmas was seeing the love and generosity of all our friends," she continued. "After living in the city for so many years, it was wonderful to be here with you, my two dear sisters, in a special town like Acorn Hill. I really knew I was home where I belong."

"We never doubted you belong here," Alice said. "I remember the amazing response you had to the cookie drive. Everyone wanted to help."

"Or knew someone who needed a visit," Louise said. "We found out there are lots of great bakers in Acorn Hill."

"That's for sure. And it has been nice to see different groups take on the drive each year since. This year the Methodists teamed up with members of the City Council to host it."

"Did you read Duke Gladstone's story in the *Acorn Nutshell* this week?" Louise asked.

"No. I haven't had a chance to read it yet," Jane said. "Did he write a story?"

"It's the story he told you that Christmas. I thought that might be what jogged your memory about that year."

"No. But I love that Carlene collected all the stories we heard that night, and she now runs a few at Christmastime as part of our town's heritage."

"I know something you don't know," Alice said with a smug smile. "She's been interviewing many of our elderly for stories they heard from their parents too. She's planning to put all the stories together in a bound book for the historical society."

"Really? That's wonderful!" Jane said.

"Just goes to show, we never know the far-reaching effects of our efforts," Alice said.

"I love looking back and seeing how the Lord has blessed us beyond anything we've done to help others," Louise said.

The three were silent for a moment, each lost in her thoughts as the flames in the fireplace died down to glowing coals.

"Our fire is almost out. Should I put on another log?" Jane asked.

Alice yawned. Louise glanced at her watch.

"Goodness. It's after midnight. I hadn't realized it was so late. And Cynthia is already sleeping, so she'll be up early."

"I think I'm ready to call it a night." Jane stood and stretched. When she did, the lovely old nativity scene in the center of the mantel caught her eye.

"I'm fading with the fire," Louise said, standing.

"But this was a wonderful way to spend Christmas Eve." She hugged Jane and reached to encompass Alice, who joined them in a group hug.

"Merry Christmas, dear sisters," Alice said. "I've loved spending this night with you and our memories."

"Me too. But wait," Jane said, stepping back. She turned to the doorway. "I'll be right back. Don't leave yet." She hurried into the hall, opened the desk drawer, retrieved a small cloth-wrapped package and then returned to the living room. She walked to the fireplace, unwrapped the cloth and reverently placed the baby Jesus in the manger of the nativity scene.

"Happy Birthday, Jesus," she said softly as she stepped back. She heard Louise and Alice singing quietly behind her, their voices blending in sweet harmony.

"'Away in a manger, no crib for his bed, the little Lord Jesus lay down his sweet head...'"

"'The stars in the sky look down where he lay,'" Jane joined in, surprisingly on key, though a little hoarse with emotion.

"'The little Lord Jesus, asleep on the hay...'"

The Howard sisters watched the fire burn down for a minute more, then, together, they headed upstairs.

Everyone in Acorn Hill has a favorite Christmas cookie recipe. Here are a few that appeared at Jane's cookie swap for you to try at home.

Scottish Shortbread

1 cup rice flour

3 cups all-purpose flour

4 teaspoons salt

1 cup (2 sticks) butter
  (don't substitute margarine)

¾ cup superfine sugar

2 egg yolks

1/3 cup plus 1 teaspoon milk

2 tablespoons dried orange zest*
  (Rub between fingers to break into fine pieces)

Cut butter into small cubes and place in bowl of stand mixer. Sift together flours and salt, then cut into butter on low speed. (Also can be done with a pastry cutter.) Mixture should resemble a coarse meal. Add sugar until mixed, then gradually add egg yolks and milk. Add orange zest last.

Knead dough until pliable. Press into greased 9x13-inch pan or two 9-inch pie pans. Press in with thumbs until soft and even. Brick the top with a fork (pressing tines lightly into surface). Score top for cutting into small squares or wedges if using pie pans. Makes about 4½ dozen shortbread squares.

Preheat oven to 300 degrees. Bake for 50–60 minutes. You can either add topping during last half hour of baking or sprinkle with superfine sugar when still hot out of the oven.

*To make orange zest, wash an orange, then grate the outer skin. (Don't use white pulp, which is bitter.) Let grated skin dry until crisp and easily crushed.

Topping:

1 egg yolk, beaten
3 tablespoons brown sugar
¼ cup finely chopped pecans
2 teaspoons fine orange zest (optional)

Mix together and spread on top of half-baked short-bread. Return to oven and finish baking.

White Chocolate Hermits
with Eggnog Glaze

½ cup butter

½ cup shortening

2 cups sugar

3 eggs

½ teaspoon baking soda, dissolved in
   3 tablespoons milk

1 teaspoon vanilla

6 cups flour

½ teaspoon nutmeg

½ teaspoon allspice (optional)

1 teaspoon cinnamon

¼ teaspoon white pepper

1 cup white chocolate chips

1 cup dried cranberries or cherries,
   chopped and dusted with flour
   to coat

Cream together butter and shortening. (Best to use a stand mixer as dough will get thick.) Gradually add sugar and blend until creamy. Add eggs, one at a time, then milk/baking soda mixture and vanilla.

Sift the flour with the spices. Add gradually to creamed ingredients while mixing at medium speed. When completely blended, add white chocolate chips and chopped dried cranberries.

Preheat oven to 400 degrees. Grease cookie sheets. Roll walnut-size balls of dough and press down with fingers to approx. ½ inch thick. (These cookies do not spread as they cook.) Bake 8–10 minutes to a pale golden color.

Glaze:

Mix ½ cup powdered sugar and 2–3 tablespoons eggnog to a syrupy consistency. Drizzle with teaspoon and spread on top of each warm cookie with back of spoon to coat top. Let glaze dry before packing away cookies.

Mocha Krinkles

½ cup plus 2 teaspoons coconut oil
 (you can use butter, but this adds to distinct flavor)

⅔ cup unsweetened dark cocoa

1–1½ teaspoons instant coffee
 (one individual packet)

2 cups sugar

4 eggs

2 teaspoons vanilla

3 cups flour

2 teaspoons baking powder

½ teaspoon salt

Coating:
½ cup granulated sugar in a bowl
1 cup powdered sugar in a shallow bowl

Cream together oil, cocoa, coffee granules and sugar; then blend in eggs, one at a time, and vanilla. Beat until creamy.

Sift flour, baking powder, and salt. Add gradually to creamy mixture, beating on medium speed until all flour is blended in. Mixture will be stiff, but sticky. Refrigerate, covered, for several hours, until dough can be handled. Form walnut-size balls and roll first in granulated sugar, then in powdered sugar, to coat. (Granulated sugar helps keep powdered sugar from being absorbed during cooking.)

Place cookies on greased sheets, two inches apart. Cookies will spread a little.

Preheat oven to 350 degrees. Bake 10–12 minutes. Don't undercook. Cookies should cool to be crisp on the outside and soft on the inside.

Tales from Grace Chapel Inn

Once you visit the charming village of Acorn Hill, you'll never want to leave. Here, the three Howard sisters reunite after their father's death and turn the family home into a bed-and-breakfast. They rekindle old memories, rediscover the bonds of sisterhood, revel in the blessings of friendship and meet many fascinating guests along the way.